THE OBVIOUS CHILD

THE OBVIOUS CHILD

Matt Shaw

Exile Editions

Publishers of singular
Fiction, Poetry, Drama, Non-fiction and Graphic Books

2007

Library and Archives Canada Cataloguing in Publication

Shaw, Matt, 1982-

The obvious child / Matt Shaw.

ISBN 978-1-55096-082-2

I. Title.

PS8637.H384O29 2007 C813'.6 C2007-904806-4

Design and Composition by Homunculus ReproSet
Typeset in Bembo and Garamond at the Moons of Jupiter Studios
Printed in Canada by Friesens

The publisher would like to acknowledge the financial assistance of
The Canada Council for the Arts, and the Ontario Arts Council–which is an
agency of the Government of Ontario.

Conseil des Arts du Canada   Canada Council for the Arts

**ONTARIO ARTS COUNCIL
CONSEIL DES ARTS DE L'ONTARIO**

Published in Canada in 2007 by Exile Editions Ltd.
144483 Southgate Road 14
General Delivery
Holstein, Ontario, N0G 2A0
info@exileeditions.com
www.ExileEditions.com

Canadian Sales Distribution:
McArthur & Company
c/o Harper Collins
1995 Markham Road
Toronto, ON M1B 5M8
toll free: 1 800 387 0117

U.S. Sales Distribution:
Independent Publishers Group
814 North Franklin Street
Chicago, IL 60610
www.ipgbook.com
toll free: 1 800 888 4741

for Ernie & Lise, who deserve 'zhili bhili'

William James describes a man who got the [vision of truth] from laughing-gas; whenever he was under its influence, he knew the secret of the universe, but when he came to, he had forgotten it. At last, with immense effort, he wrote down the secret before the vision had faded. When completely recovered, he rushed to see what he had written. It was: "A smell of petroleum prevails throughout."

— BERTRAND RUSSELL

MATCHBOOK FOR
A MOTHER'S HAIR

Where do I start, my name is Gordon Ween.

I am seventeen and three-quarters. Three quarters is three fingers out of four fingers, or three fingers over four fingers. Seventeen means that I have seventeen wholes—which I learned is sixteen groups of four fingers out of four fingers.

Mother played cards. There was Mrs. Baker, Mrs. Gingrinch and Mrs. Lowell. In the afternoon, at a table in my house, they played Yuke Her. I do not know how to play Yuke Her but I watched them every afternoon. When they played they tried to yuke each other, Mother and Mrs. Baker would look at the numbers they held in their hands and add them up and sort the pairs, and Mrs. Lowell leaned over Mrs. Gingrinch and then leaned back and then someone would lay cards down and Mrs. Lowell mumbled a dirty word and Mother scolded her, not in front of Gordon, don't say those things in front of Gordon, she said. Then the cards were down and Mrs. Lowell and Mrs. Gingrinch would be happy. On the table were cards with coloured shapes and unhappy faces, the shapes of shovels and hearts.

The house? The house was my house. The table was round and pretty, there were red flowers with thick stems in a bowl. It was an eating bowl, not a flower bowl. It was low and wide, for soup, but Mother always cut the stems and sat the petals in the bowl so there were no stems. They were coloured little heads, especially when they were tulips, and they got darker and darker until they curled and new heads were on the table for Yuke Her. As the heads turned dark and sad, their smell eroded and the bowl dried out. There were four black chairs around the big table, but my chair was by the window looking at the four big chairs. The window drapes were the colour of hedges and there were no dishes in the sink.

There were always bottles on the table, green with purple labels and Mrs. Gingrinch always laughed when she said we almost don't need the flowers on the table, these bottles are flowers themselves and make us bloom when we drink she said, and she giggled as she looked at me sitting in my chair.

My chair, I sat on a chair beside the table. It was my chair, I always sat in it, and it was red. It fit my back and Mother liked it because it always makes you sit up straight, Gordon, you never sit straight enough. People will not like you if don't sit straight, Gordon, what will Mrs. Lowell and Mrs. Gingrinch think of you if you slouch, Gordon.

Oh no, Mrs. Lowell said, don't listen to her. You know I like you, you know how much I like you, I've shown you how I like you you know that. She never said that when Mother was there, when Mother was there she said nonsense, Rette, you'll hurt the poor boy's feelings. Gordon is absolutely wonderful, we all love Gordon.

Did you know the pretty parts of flowers are the reproductive organs, said Mrs. Baker.

They're certainly more used than yours, said Mrs. Gingrinch, you're ugly.

I am not, said Mrs Baker, her best friend.

Gordon, said Mrs. Gingrinch, don't listen to your mother. She's turning red because all day she loses all she has to us. Terrible. She's terrible.

Mother glared at her.

See, said Mrs. Gingrinch, she doesn't laugh at it because it's true, Gordon. Mrs. Baker and your mother never win together.

I don't cheat, and we win sometimes, said Mrs. Baker. It's not true.

You know it is, said Mrs. Gingrinch, you take from Rette too. I never won when I played with you, either. But Rette never stops playing with you and she never understands our faces.

I understand there's nothing else to understand in your faces, said Mother.

If you understood any faces, you would understand Mrs. Baker's, said Mrs. Gingrinch. Her face is so plain she cannot lie. Even when she puts on her mascara and makeup you know she is trying to hide her thoughts. When she tries to hide her thoughts you know exactly what they are. But you can't see that, said Mrs. Gingrinch, and we can so we win.

My face is not plain, said Mrs. Baker.

It is so, said Mrs. Gingrinch.

I do not wear makeup to hide things. I wear it to look pretty, said Mrs. Baker.

Hmm, said Mrs. Gingrinch.

Mrs. Gingrinch and Mrs. Baker were best friends. They fought all the time at Yuke Her, Mrs. Baker accusing Mrs. Gingrinch of cheating and Mrs. Gingrinch calling Mrs. Baker too plain, she said a face that ugly should be much better at hiding things. Mrs. Baker is ugly, she looks like a squirrel I saw a dog catch from a tree. I would never say she looked like a squirrel from my chair because I wasn't supposed to talk from the chair I was supposed to watch for cheating.

If I talked Mother always told me to stop talking. Everything was good until I talked so I didn't. That's why I never said that Mrs. Baker looked like a fly I hit with a newspaper that crawled on its broken legs or that Mrs. Gingrinch sometimes farted when she took me upstairs to show me every week. Even though I knew what she wanted to show me I wanted to see again and I wanted to tell everyone at the table that all of them, except Mother, showed me the same thing all the time but only Mrs. Gingrinch smelled when she showed me, and I thought that was funny. They looked funny when they climbed on me to show me what they called love. When I talked it was never bad until Mrs. Gingrinch, Mrs. Lowell and Mrs. Baker went home. Then Mother would drink more of the bottles with the purple labels and stand up.

Wait for me in your chair, Gordon. I mean it.

So I sat and didn't say no because it would make it worse.

There are reasons I ask you not to talk, Gordon, but you didn't listen. You remember what we do every time you do talk when I tell you not to. I would never hurt you, Gordon, but you have to understand this

Gordon, even if it is the only thing you understand. You have problems, Gordon, but you're not a completely stupid boy.

For each thing I said while she yuked her friends she plucked one hair from my head and she tickled my face. Here's another one, she'd say. Her lighter was the colour of a fire engine like my chair. She held the hair up to my nose and flicked the lighter and held the lighter to the scared hair.

I do this for your good, Gordon. Other mothers will hit their kids, I only make you sit here and ask you not to talk. If you talk I make you smell your hair burning. This will teach you that I love you and will make you a smarter boy than you are. It could be worse, Gordon. Other mothers don't love their children but I love mine. We could be poor or we could die in a fire ourselves and smell like this, this is what you will smell like if you are on fire, said Mother. It could be worse. Fire would be worse.

What did it smell like? I do not like to remember, I like Mrs. Lowell, Mrs. Gingrinch, Mrs. Baker, but mostly Mrs. Lowell.

Mrs. Lowell, Mrs. Gingrinch, Mrs. Baker never burned my hair. Mother never talked about burning my hair at Yuke Her. They drank and laughed and they looked at me with eyes that made me smell smoke and matchbooks when they lit their cigarettes and drank from the bottles. They played every morning and they finished before I was supposed to eat.

Mother did this on purpose. Gordon, she said, today I want you to walk Mrs. Baker home. Then you can eat your lunch, I will make you mashed potatoes and a sandwich, a tuna sandwich, dress warm it's snowing outside, she said. I don't like tuna sandwiches but I never said that I don't like tuna sandwiches because I'm not allowed to talk in my red chair, just watch for cheating. I walked Mrs. Baker or Mrs. Gingrinch or Mrs. Lowell home every day and we walked slowly so I would not have to eat the tuna sandwich until I got home and if it took longer then it would be longer before I ate the sandwich. Mrs. Baker went home on Monday and Wednesday and Mrs. Gingrinch went home on Tuesday. I always walked fast with Mrs. Baker because on Wednesday Mother would make me mashed potatoes and no tuna and I like mashed potatoes. Mrs. Baker is ugly and I do not like to walk with her anyway so I walk fast. On Thursday and Friday and Saturday I walked Mrs. Lowell home and Mother and Mrs. Gingrinch and Mrs. Baker stayed at the Yuke Her table and drank from the bottles all day. I walked slow on these days because I did not want to go back to the house when they had the bottles empty.

Who was first? It was Mrs. Lowell who first showed me things. That day we walked fast because Mrs. Lowell was walking fast and looking at the watch on her hand. It was ten after twelve, which means that we had fifty minutes until one o'clock because there are sixty minutes in one hour and twenty-four hours in one day.

Why are we walking fast, I asked Mrs. Lowell.

Because, she said, I don't have too much time and there's something I need to show you. It's cold, Gordon. It's January. Aren't you cold?

It is wrong to be cold. Show me, I said.

I can't show you here but I will show you. It's a thank-you for walking me home.

We are walking too fast.

If we are not fast I will not be able to show you because someone will come home. Besides it is very cold and you're not dressed properly. Why doesn't Rette dress you better.

I did not know other people lived with Mrs. Lowell. I never heard about other people when they played Yuke Her. It was twelve-thirty when we got to her white house, which means we had thirty minutes to one o'clock. Inside she sat me at the kitchen table, I sat at a chair, a chair different from mine. It is not red but tall.

Can you show me what it is, I like surprises I said.

She bit the corner of my ear her brown hair smelled like mangos and she wore purple rings on her fingers ice, and there isn't any time, face icicles that fell from the roof as she touched me and shattered into pieces glass prisms her rings grey purple with red amethysts she moaned I screamed she took me upstairs to the bed lie there and don't move, there isn't any time, don't move the bed shook I shook isn't any time I never felt it before it was powerful as the hairs lit in my face does my mother do this do this I screamed don't move she screamed Mother doesn't do this to me and we both moved and then the hair split and the clock on the bedside table wasn't counting anymore and then there wasn't any time and she sped up and then I didn't move and it was finished and there wasn't any more time and I didn't move.

I didn't talk because I didn't want to make Mrs. Lowell angry. She was not angry she was glowing and her mouth didn't smell so dirty now, so much like the smoke when she was in Mother's house. She was on her back on the green sheet the colour of hedges. Her feet were sweating. She smelled like mangos and cigarettes.

Do you know what that was, she said.

I did not want to answer because I did not want to be wrong. I don't know anything.

Did you like what I showed you, she said.

She put her hand on me and rubbed her palm against me and said you are very good. I just wanted you to lie still and you did and it was wonderful. You made me feel so good.

Your feet are sweaty, I said.

Next time we walk home I will show you something else, she said. You can never tell your mother that I show you things. She wouldn't understand and then I couldn't show you anymore. You have to be quiet. You have to go because Mr. Lowell will be home and you can't be here when Mr. Lowell gets here.

Her feet were moving and rubbing me. The smell of mangos was flying out of the window and Mrs. Lowell made the clock move again.

We are lovely and beautiful but your mother has never understood lovely and beautiful. She understands nothing about faces.

I wanted to leave.

No, she was not the only one, the other women at the game too. Mother told me to walk Mrs. Gingrinch home. It was winter still. Mrs. Gingrinch never said she was going to show me anything and we walked slow so I did not know anything.

Mrs. Gingrinch lives in a small house with a garage. It is white with tiny windows. The curtains are the colour of toothpaste, red white green, you can see them through the window. The shutters are blue. It was so pretty I wanted to go inside.

Are we going inside, I said.

No, we are going to go in the garage.

I'm cold, I said, I'd like some hot chocolate inside.

No, sweetie, you can't go inside. Mr. Gingrinch is upstairs in bed, sick. You can't come inside, Gordon. But you can come warm up in the garage before you go home. We can sit in the car. The garage will be warm. You like cars, all boys like cars.

The garage was not pretty. There was nothing there I wanted to see and it was grey and the car was too small for my knees.

I said, I don't fit, my knees are too big. Why can't I have any hot chocolate and then she touched me, like Mrs. Lowell. This is different now it knows she pulled the seats back and climbed on top and it was noisy the sounds of saws and wood the sound of pain and work and effort and the vice clamps closed and it was noisy and she moaned and I screamed and it was nothing new but it was and she said move, why aren't you moving so I moved a little but the car was too small for me to move and she moved more than me it hurt like a saw might hurt like a nail like a chain like a lawnmower on my belly and 'me' parts and I screamed and she screamed louder and all I wanted was a hot chocolate and it was the sound of work and effort it was all sounds and Mr. Gingrinch was in the house somewhere and then she started making farting and she said don't laugh don't stop and it was the sound of work and effort and a lawnmower on my me parts. When she was finished showing me she fell asleep in the back seat and I sat beside her watching the clock in the garage. It was ten after one, which meant there were fifty minutes until two o'clock.

Now when they played Yuke Her it was different to me. Mrs. Baker was still ugly, Mrs. Gingrinch still called Mrs. Baker ugly. Mother still drank and burned my hair under my nose when I came home. A horrible smell, like Mrs. Gingrinch's smells but the same the same.

Rette, that's cheating, said Mrs. Lowell. She slammed the cards on the table.

I am not cheating, said Mother. I made my own son watch to show there is no cheating. If I was cheating Gordon would've said something, wouldn't you, Gordon.

I didn't say anything. If I did Mother would burn hair under my nose.

That doesn't matter, said Mrs. Gingrinch, you're taking advantage of us, you and Mrs. Baker.

I don't know what's going on, said Mrs. Baker.

That's because nothing is going on, said Mother.

That's because you're ugly, Mrs. Gingrinch said.

I'm not ugly, said Mrs. Baker.

Mother knocked the flower heads on the floor and the low wide bowl broke into pieces. Mrs. Gingrinch shook a bottle with a purple label shouting this is ridiculous, this is ridiculous while Mrs. Lowell bent over to pick up the shards of the vase.

Don't get up, Gordon, she said, you'll hurt your feet.

Get up, Gordon, and clean your mess, said Mother.

Gordon should do the work, said Mrs. Gingrinch to Mrs. Lowell. He never does anything, he just lies there.

Why should he do anything, said Mrs. Lowell, this is not his fault, he is not his fault. You leave him alone, it's not his fault who he is.

I walked Mrs. Lowell home. It was snowing it was sunny. We walked slow but when we got there we went upstairs and Mrs. Lowell told me that I was so good at lying still, she liked it best when I lay still and she moved and I liked it that she liked it. I did not want to think about Mother burning my hair there is all the time in the world she screamed and I did not I know there is a pattern a nice pattern and I lie still there is all the time in the world but I still don't move the smell I notice most is Mrs. Lowell's feet and my sweat much more pleasant than Mrs. Gingrinch in the car and much better to look all the time in the world at than ugly Mrs. Baker and I screamed and that made her scream louder and louder and the more I lay still the more she moved and when she finished I was sure there was all the time in the world.

I liked that she liked it, I liked her better than Mrs. Baker. I don't want to tell you about Mrs. Baker, with Mrs. Baker it felt dirty it was not fun then, not fun or warm it was almost as bad as the fire and hair. Mrs. Baker never took me home, we just went to a park. It was so cold and I wanted hot chocolate but knew I wouldn't get any.

Why, I don't want to talk about it. It's not special.

She threw herself under a tree, take me now she said.

I didn't understand. She grabbed me and pulled me under. The snow was soft and cold under my knees. She had a green hood and that made it better but it was so hard the sun was on my back and the wind bit my face not warm with Mrs. Lowell not work with Mrs. Gingrinch just empty like the bottles on the Yuke Her table, empty like the numbers on the cards, empty like the lighter Mother owned it was too much work and she screamed a little bit but I never said anything I knew I was doing it now and it was just doing not like Mrs. Lowell Mrs. Baker was not anything she was like Mother said ugly people are empty inside it was hard I knew what I was doing but it was empty.

I did not like when Mrs. Baker did that with me, but not because she was ugly. She was ugly, but she was empty. Mrs. Gingrinch was empty too, Mother was empty, Mrs. Lowell was not empty. And when it happened again every day it never felt better with Mrs. Gingrinch or Mrs. Baker, it felt awful and wrong, like cheating at Yuke Her.

When they played Yuke Her now it was awful. They were always fighting. I sat and did not talk while Mother and Mrs. Lowell Mrs. Gingrinch Mrs. Baker threw the flowers and the bottles and screamed and it was horrible and when it was all over I didn't get tuna any more. They didn't talk about me but they looked at me when they fought and I sat with my hands on the knees of my pants in the red chair at the window. Mother kept shouting at me, speak, Gordon, you son of a bitch, tell them I am not cheating, I just want to win and win. I win, everyone gets angry with me you dumb shit, you retard, speak.

Rette, not in front of Gordon, said Mrs. Lowell. It's your own fault for cheating.

Mrs. Baker said, I'm not cheating, Rette, it's you, I'm sick of losing with you.

Mother hit Mrs. Baker and she had the same look on her ugly nose she had when I finished at the park. I said that's the same look you had at the park and Mrs. Baker looked at me with scared eyes but no one else heard me. Mother threw the bowl at Mrs. Lowell and hit her in the face. The flowers fell everywhere on the floor and Mrs. Lowell screamed a different scream. Blood came through the fingers on her face and ran down her and she put it in her hair when she tried to push the hair off her face. She left a trail of blood. Mother stopped and Mrs. Baker cried and Mrs. Gingrinch had her hair in a mess.

I walked with Mrs. Gingrinch. I did not want her, I wanted Mrs. Lowell but now Mrs. Lowell would never come back again she would never have a face again. It was not mine but it was pretty and she was better than Mrs. Gingrinch or Mrs. Baker. Mrs. Lowell.

I was angry. At the house we went to the garage. I did not want hot chocolate. She pulled me into the car and turned the car on. There was the sound of the radio. Mr. Gingrinch is upstairs, sick, asleep she said. I told him someone was coming to fix the car today there could be as much noise as she wanted. She said she really needed it now. I was angry and I wanted to hurt her, she was so mean and empty as empty as Mother.

I touched her first. She moaned and touched me you are going to move she said to me that is wonderful and I moved I was so angry I was like nails a saw a car engine and she scratched my back and bit my ear and I moved I moved I moved I did not lie still and I thought about Mrs. Lowell I wanted to cry I wanted to make Mrs. Gingrinch cry and scream and scratch me harder because I was moving after she told me not to but Mrs. Gingrinch was screaming and holding me all the time in the world because Mrs. Lowell would never come back it was two-thirty which means that there is forever before Mrs. Lowell comes back and tells me to be still. Her head moves everywhere and I grab her hair it is three o'clock which means we have been in the garage for thirty minutes.

You were incredible, she said, you moved so much, oh my god.

She fell asleep on the back seat and I started to cry I felt so bad. I don't know what I felt it was worse than the burning hair or Mother throwing the vase at Mrs.

Lowell. I was so cold and empty, Mrs. Gingrinch and Mrs. Baker were so awful and empty. I got out of the car and closed the door softly and closed the garage door when I left so Mrs. Gingrinch could have her nap in the garage and I went to the park. When I got home Mrs. Baker was gone. Mother made me tuna but no mashed potatoes and she burned a whole patch of my hair in front of my face and screamed.

You were so bad today, Gordon, shame on you, don't you understand what you're doing, I asked you to talk and you didn't.

Mother, I don't know what to do, I cried, you hit Mrs. Lowell I am just supposed to sit by the window and tell you if people are cheating.

You don't even understand what you're doing, you're a dumb boy, Gordon. A dumb boy and you don't even do well by me and if you don't do well by me then those women don't deserve your kindness, they're mean dumb bitches and we don't need them. You are a burden, Gordon, a mule. You are good for nothing more than watching your mother play cards and being stupid. Those women don't like you, Gordon, they wanted you to say I cheat all the time at Yuke Her.

I do not know what else to tell you. I do not know what else. I don't know why you keep asking me about

Mrs. Gingrinch. Mrs. Gingrinch is empty. I don't understand you, why you ask me about what happened to Mrs. Gingrinch. This story is not Mrs. Gingrinch's story, it's Mrs. Lowell's. This is about Mrs. Lowell, where is she. I told you about mother and my chair. The car you put me in never takes me home. Where is Mrs. Lowell, I told you about my chair.

TENDLE & OSLO

Tendle did not bring home the dog because she had a vision of the perfect family, as was her husband's thought. The dog was very tall with thin, grey legs. He had the body of a Great Dane, but his snout was speckled and sharp. He was a very ugly dog, her husband said, and Tendle agreed with him on that count. At the shelter he was the most forlorn, his big head tucked between his paws, his body a hopeless sprawl on the concrete. Sophocles, the dog, was nine years old and very quiet. The first night was solemn. Oslo had no questions about the animal, no admonitions or grievances or questions. He believed he knew everything, and Tendle gave the dog his privacy so he might become acclimated to the imperfect family.

Oslo had for many years in bed laid his arm across Tendle's back as though to keep her in place. But tonight she rested at the bed's edge, her arm resting on the belly of the dog on the floor beside her. Her husband's arm lay in the emptiness between the two bodies upon the sheets. Oslo could wake without disturbing his wife, and the thought of such morning peace lulled him. The dog woke with Oslo, but never left the embrace of Tendle's arm. Oslo drank long cups of coffee at the table alone, with the newspaper underneath his feet and stared out the window before he drove to work.

Oslo was of retirement age but he stayed at the pressing plant because it was a good wage and somewhere to go. *Why do you need to go anywhere,* Tendle wanted to ask her husband, *what is wrong with right here in this house?* She asked instead the wise Sophocles, who made her mornings much less lonely. The dog never answered but grew livelier in the house with each day, and the horrible questions Tendle wanted to ask were lost in the joy of her new friendship. He fetched balls and sat at her feet and moaned to be let out the door to pee. With her husband gone, the oppressive weight of the kitchen vanished. The house grew warm.

Oslo had made it clear there was little he wished to share with her, although she had many fears herself and no one in whom to confide. Her hair, which fell across her eyes in a boyish brown mop like a young Beatle, failed to age alongside her face. In the mirror she looked neither old nor young. What was she then? The common denominator of her assessment was *not*: she was *not* Tendle. The dog thought the logic was sound. Whenever she thought these sad thoughts he sat beside her, staring into her face. What was this dog, neither a Great Dane nor a cattle hound?

Tendle's eyes were crumbling into caves, and the tip of her nose had grown into a bulb, seemingly without cartilage to hold it in place. Her teeth loosened from general neglect. She brushed, but not nearly enough. She could wiggle them with her tongue. She could fold her ears against the sides of her head, or pull down the loose jowls around her thin mouth. She proved to herself she could look the part of *not* Tendle, too. With Sophocles at her side she felt comfortable exploring the dark recesses of her face, exposing the wrinkles and crevices beneath the hundred-watt bulb.

Oslo never tolerated such narcissistic preening. He had once asked Tendle, shortly after they were married, to remove all the mirrors in the house. Tendle knew then how to handle Oslo, who was already mildly perturbed. It was silly and she told him why. The mirrors in the house stayed, but Oslo grumbled. When she looked in the mirror these mornings, Tendle couldn't help but wonder whether such was the event setting all of Oslo's future cantankerousness. When Oslo saw Tendle exploring herself, pushing her teeth with her tongue, he reproached his wife as an owner does a puppy.

Brush them, Tendle, damn it, he said. *Don't wiggle them, you'll make them come out sooner.*

Of course, I brush, she said. *Don't be ridiculous and hurtful.*

I haven't seen you brush in fifteen years, he said.

You haven't barged uninvited into the bathroom in fifteen years.

I have so!

You have not and you know it, your common decency—your manners, although such a word seems archaic with you—have given you that one tic of gentlemanliness. And, she added, *that is ridiculous, that wiggling them will make them come out sooner. They will come when they do; that they are is no secret. And the sooner you see it, Oslo, the better for us both.*

But to Oslo the situation was not worth discussing, and so Tendle learned to walk back through the bedroom in the dark, stepping over the sleeping mass of Sophocles, who always lay in the same place. When she slept she kept her hand on his belly, and her husband's arm fell in the space between their bodies.

Because Oslo began to rise earlier than his wife, the number of such arguments that occurred in the morning disappeared. He would finish his bathroom business before the sun had even begun to rise, heaving itself from the earth and ascending through its daily morning ritual. He thought the morning sun was as ugly as his wife's loose teeth. He drank his coffee and read the paper, but reading so early in the morning, when the sunlight was still depressingly grey upon the newsprint, gave him headaches. He turned to the TV news but it was ostentatious; the morning talk shows banal; the weather network predictable; the sports scores empty numbers; the DOW Jones stock a pendulum, predictably *pendumulous*.

These early mornings, on days off from the press, Oslo put his hands to work, however little he knew about building things. He constructed lopsided eavestroughs that formed a craggy, rough-hewn perimeter around the house. He planted a garden of green peppers and tomato plants in cones. (Only half the garden ever bloomed, being the only half he got around to planting.) He built a doghouse of cheap pine. It seemed ridiculous to him at that time, but what an omen it would become later, with the necessity of many more doghouses. He renovated the porch, he worked the yard and pulled weeds, he insulated the attic. He did these things as long as he could bear and then he left them. He cared little if he finished or was successful.

Tendle thought her husband was improving himself. With Oslo in the garage or the yard, her own morning ritual was unimpeded. The sun rose vigorously. She wiggled her teeth joyously in the mirror. How malleable! How playful! How unutterably *young* wiggling her teeth made her feel! She felt like a twelve-year-old girl who dreamed of marriage and play ovens and first dances with boys doused in their fathers' cologne. She imagined her hymen was intact again. How like the sun it would burn! She blushed. She wiggled her teeth.

Such youth was not what her husband noticed. It wasn't about the brushing of course, but the widening gap between himself and his wife that he saw that morning when she wiggled her teeth in the mirror: her receding beauty, the apnea that blocked her sinuses and lungs, the tiny pain he felt between his testicles when he awoke from sleep. The chores weren't done out of thoroughness but fear, which was that everything he loved (which was only Tendle) was leaving him, like a bottle pulled by the tide into the ocean.

What Oslo was learning in the yard was how to build quietly. Hammers didn't ring, and cords of wood never hit the ground with heavy thuds. The saws were muffled. Tendle, upon discovering the doghouse (and wondering whether its intent was as gift or banishment for Sophocles) was aghast that her husband had completed the task under her nose without discovery. Oslo said, with a smile, that the first doghouse had been built without once waking the dog. Oslo was right: Tendle had never taken her hand off the old boy's belly before she rose in the morning. The doghouse was a single completed project among dozens, and the house looked like gothic architecture without the beauty. Scaffolding lined the house and mounds of dirt for the garden sat at the end of the driveway.

Convinced that the changes were something like progress (stiff old Oslo maneuvering those boards like a young carpenter!), Tendle brought home one dog and then another. At the end, Tendle had fourteen dogs. All were a mottled blending of two entirely unique dogs (in the best cases, mutts themselves) into one unidentifiable mongrel. What was said in the silence of that first night that had led them here?

With so many dogs Tendle could no longer keep her eyes or hands on them, and the animals varied wildly in ages and dispositions. When she woke and saw the newest mess in the garage or yard, she surveyed the evidence to surmise exactly *who*, dog or man, had caused the scene. Yet, despite the chaos, Oslo was calm and made little insult about the dogs. He was calm and at peace. Tendle thought it best not to question him.

She lost her teeth one by one. If they fell into her mouth she was careful not to swallow, and placed them in her night side table in an old ring box. Sometimes she woke to feel a new space between her teeth. Where had the tooth gone? It was very important to her that Oslo never saw a thing, perhaps causing the temporal peace to implode. And if she could not find the tooth between the sheets she looked down at Sophocles (despite all the new companions, he slept in the same spot he always had), who stared at her as if to say *What tooth, Tendle? It is all taken care of.* Oslo, now masterfully silent and phantasmagorical, might burst in the room at the any moment, and Tendle always felt relief at a prompt discovery or Sophocles' assurances. She was learning to be discreet herself, making tiny spitballs out of paper, sticking them between the gaps, and taking supreme effort not to smile too widely during emergencies, a fairly easy task with solemn Oslo. When Oslo was at work she visited the orthodontist and had dentures fixed, and paid with money she had stashed in the nightstand drawer beside the ring box. She was careful to make sure the dentures were white, but not too white, straight, but not too much so.

Oslo worked diligently at the doghouses. Perhaps the completion of the first spurred him on, or perhaps he saw some improvement in his workmanship that helped his self-esteem. None of the following doghouses were an obvious improvement on the ones that came before. Some were taller, or wider, depending on the dog, and the colours or grains of the planks rarely matched. When he finished the latest doghouse, he carried it out back and set it next to the previous in a long row across the back-yard. With every doghouse he placed beside another Oslo had to admit, sadly, that each doghouse in the row made the others look less natural and at ease, a contradiction. *Who had ever seen six, seven, twelve doghouses in a single small backyard?* But there were two more to finish. And there was the siding, and the eavestroughs, planting the other half of the garden, clearing out the garage, the necessary yard sales: there was a life's work and less than a life to do it in.

Some of the dogs slept in the yard. They were free to go where they pleased through a pet door, and in the mornings Oslo always saw snouts poking out from the doorways. Inevitably there were far fewer snouts than doghouses, most of the dogs preferring the warm carpet of the main house. But there were some who desired solitude and independence, and these Oslo liked best. They enjoyed his work, and he them; when he built the doghouses he tried to keep watch and avoided waking these companions. However, Sophocles never left Tend-le's side, and his doghouse (one of the smallest and most askew) was never inhabited by any dog. Its roof was, at the front, flat and wide, and Oslo used it as a bench when he tired in the morning, sipping a cup of coffee.

Who is Oslo now, Tendle thought one night as she went to sleep, Oslo's space beside her vacant. *At work is he the same old Oslo? What pleasure does he derive from the doghouses, or the dogs?* She tucked the blankets tight around her; Oslo's side of the bed was perfect. He might never have been there. Yet, inside, Tendle still felt like a perpetual housewife. Her desire for perfection still ached. *And when will Oslo come to bed?* But she did not know. She fell asleep.

When she woke she lay not on her side of the bed but Oslo's. To her dismay, her arm was not on the belly of Sophocles. He was not in his space. There was only a collection of mottled hairs on the throw rug. She threw herself off the bed and the comforter dropped to the floor. He was not in the washroom and she paid scant attention to the mirror. The dentures were tucked in their solution in the bedside table. In her anxiety she nearly forgot to wrap a robe around her waist.

She stumbled down the steps. There were some dogs in the kitchen, and two in the living room, their varying shades of grey and brown and black spotted across the purple couches. But none was the large and beautiful

Sophocles. She ran into the yard. Snouts peered at her from doghouses, but none raised at the smell of the unusual morning visitor. Which house had Oslo built for Sophocles? *That must be it.* She ran down the row, peering into the round and square and oblong doorways of each house. She saw blue and green eyes, long and short snouts; some animals thumped their tails against the walls.

She peeked into the furthest doghouse, which looked as though it must have been the first. The roof did not fit properly and in between the seams and joints were gaps and cracks. She put her hand on the roof to steady herself as she knelt. She felt a sliver pierce her skin and the house rocked loosely under her weight. There was no dog inside and it smelled as though there had never been.

Tendle! Tendle! Good morning!

She heard Oslo's shouts behind her and rose. How quiet he was! He was dressed in a white, buttoned shirt, his hair slicked against his head with thick pomade. He wore black shoes and black socks, and he had Sophocles by the collar. The great dog pulled hard toward Tendle and dragged Oslo with him. Tendle saw sweat stains forming under his white shirt. It was such an unusual sight, Oslo dressed so well, and an unusual sound, Oslo moving so ghostly, that she gaped her gummy mouth at him. Stunned, Oslo released the collar and began to shriek as the dog lavished Tendle with kisses.

ANECDOTE
OF
THE JAR

Coo found the jar everywhere. He plucked it from Madeleine's hair when he had one of her great tits cupped purple in the other hand. When he dug out the septic tank after a disastrous overflow he discovered it in a moist and stinking pile of earth. It rattled under the hood of the Datsun, trapped between the serpentine belt which rubbed furiously against the glass. Everywhere Coo went he 'barely' found a jar: the jar was both 'barren,' bereft of any substance he could discern, and 'barely there'. He was never sure how he found it but he did many times daily and without failure. It did not fit in the pockets of his jeans so he thrust it down the front of his pants, where the jar seemed to always disappear in a moment of forgetfulness occurring as easily as the conscious effort to breathe. If he thought of it, Coo could not make himself forget the act. Yet if he attempted to live an entire day thinking, without interruption, *breathe, Coo, breathe,* he failed.

The jar was like a Mason jar; it was tall, and un-
etched. (Maybe it was not like a Mason jar at all.) It was
round, except for a blunt landing which allowed the jar
to sit upright on a shelf. When Coo found the jar it
never sat upright or proper; it lay instead on its side or
upside down, or he found it in the sugar bowl, with the
lid off, the contents filled with sugar, and the mystery
substance (or lack thereof) entirely vanished. There was
no order except that he found it everywhere: in his laundry, rattling in the washing machine, in the burnt embers
of the fireplace, so plainly on the kitchen table that he
scarcely noticed that it was *the* jar and not some other,
less significant, jar. He saw it tinkling in the coffee shop,
TIPS boldly scrawled across it. He even found it on
people: Madeleine's hair as they entangled in an aggres-
sive bout of intimacy, a massive bulge in his father's pants
which Coo desperately hoped was the jar, at a Sunday
family dinner, in a co-worker's orange hard hat, and
thoroughly entangled in his friend Paulson's fishing line
on a Sunday morning at Lake Milsen.

Coo kept this news to himself. The jar caused several emotions and at the very least he had first to decide
for himself how he felt. Initially he was surprised at its
appearance and a little charmed. *How,* he wondered,
why, who, and each *when* caused further questions. His

routine as a truck driver (he drove the same route every day, from an auto plant to an auto warehouse) was dull and uninteresting and he was glad for the sparkle of the jar. However, with each appearance Coo became more distraught. The jar never signalled a bad omen, but seeing or holding it caused Coo to consider his sanity: perhaps this jar was not real, and consequently threatened to extinguish, via an extended date in a facility for mental disorders, the very routine the jar provided an escape from. So the jar was both a good and bad omen. Mathematically these notions cancelled out and left a plain and empty jar. Although Maddy was perturbed a jar was found in her hair without explanation, and Paulson was befuddled how his lure had entangled a jar, Coo was assured the jars were harmless and said nothing to his friends.

If he was insane, he reasoned, the condition did not worsen. He saw no other jars; there could be only one jar at one time. Whenever he thought he saw a second he panicked before remembering where the first had been and that it was no longer there. He learned to control his outward responses to the jar. Madeleine and Paulson said nothing about it to him. And Coo made no mention of it to his father, whom, he hoped, never noticed the jar inside his pants or, if he had, would never mention to his son that he had inexplicably pulled a jar from his crotch. That would be worse than a kidney stone, or telling your child that the screaming in the bathroom was the result of kidney stones, both of which Coo's father had done. So they ate their dinners together as though nothing was happening even though, in a way that cannot be explained, this consciousness brought them closer.

Years passed and since the jar didn't harm Coo, it was left alone. His friends never noticed, or else thought Coo was a prankster or a neurotic. It did not affect his friendships, and he continued to drive his route. It distracted him from his work only once, when it appeared out on the highway beneath the front tire and ruptured it.

Madeleine (whom Coo suspected never recovered from the jar in her hair) broke up with him because she loved Dee, a welder from the country. After breakfast one morning Coo noticed the jar was beside his juice glass. Bored and curious again, he opened the jar, dropped in a handful of corn flakes, and resealed it. Because he wondered what would happen, it took a long time for the jar to disappear. It finally disappeared, after two years, because Coo's father passed away. In his grief, Coo finally forgot the jar.

It reappeared several days after the funeral with a note inside. Coo was ecstatic; his father's death now had meaning, and the jar had returned! The note was a little larger than a fortune from a cookie. It read 'Coo found the jar everywhere.' Coo was mystified.

Over the next several years Coo took the jar to every stranger he thought might be able to help. He could not forget the mysterious sentence, and therefore the jar never disappeared. He took it to a psychic, who pronounced that because the jar had no aura, there was nothing to predict. It took the birth of his child, Gee, to forget this jar; a letter from an old friend informing him Madeleine was dead the next; Paulson moved to Europe, and his farewell party had the same effect. The notes piled up; he again discovered the jars in strange places. Coo realized the notes were writing the abridged version of his biography.

He grew very old, and his mind was afflicted with mental illnesses. He was perfectly aware he was very old. The notes in the jar had caught up with his life. He was at the end, elderly and unable to slow the messages because of his declining mind. 'Madeleine,' read one fragment. Coo remembered Madeleine and her voluptuous hair. It caused him pain. He knew it caused him pain because the next note told him so. Her voluptuous hair.... He knew he forgot, but not what he forgot. How honest the jar was with him. He owed the jar more than he was aware. The messages kept coming, and although he forgot them, he read all but the last.

DRESCHL
& THE
OBVIOUS CHILD

Plektos Ersatz was a detective by occupation. That alone fed the curiosity of people who asked him how he earned his living. Detecting is a curious and well-known trade and so people are full of questions. In movies or drugstore paperbacks it is a thrilling career of violence and intrigue. People cannot understand the thrill of being a gun's target, or the righteousness of apprehending criminals, yet they recognize their soul in a character who seeks because they too lose things constantly, and struggle to find whatever is lost. It is not too big a stretch for ordinary people to imagine themselves apprehending a criminal when they at last find their car keys beneath the couch cushion.

Plektos Ersatz is interested in people, but only specific people; it is not useful to be interested in everyone. That task would occupy more time than the world has. Plektos, then, is interested in two broad types of people: people who are present, and people who are not. In the world of private investigation absent people are called victims or suspects. Present people are often witnesses, fact sources, people who clutch tenuously at the absentee. However, they too may be suspects. A thought plagued Ersatz as he slept in his bed with a too-lit moon casting a searchlight upon his brow: anyone at all may be a suspect, but a detective does not have the time to suspect everyone. Ersatz makes choices, and quickly, before the absentee's place in the world is shorn. This is very abstract thinking, a key quality of a detective's mind. It is also a good reason not to become a detective: to reduce one's existential stress.

Ersatz was at his desk when he had a client. It made him look permanent. As though all his power was internal, sitting at a mahogany desk with his hands clasped and waiting for someone to come in. He dressed immaculately, with properly buttoned shirts and a belt that matched his shoes. The chair had a high back and made him sit straight. He kept his desk neat, with a ruler and three pads of legal paper. He kept several filing cabinets, more than were needed, to make himself look reputable, and to use the office space. The lights buzzed. In pulpy fiction the client is always a woman.

She walked into the office like it was the setting of a *film noir.* She wore a sundress with an animal scarf across her neck. Ersatz wouldn't have been surprised if it were alive, a snake or a leopard. But he would try to not look surprised if it were.

As she walked, her bones seemed to be oddly disconnected from each other. She kept her shoulders straight to balance the weight of her head, large and round, her thick black hair piled upon her crown. Her hands were small, barely large enough to cup her own breasts. The mark of difference was a single earlobe hung lower than the other—she wore mismatched earrings. Both were rectangular, but one was larger and must have been made of a heavier alloy. Ersatz kept his hands clasped. Here is an example of a detective's work: her head's misbalanced weight, unevenly distributed across her masculine shoulders, was the cause of her discombobulated slithering into his office. The entire problem was in her head; it was physically askew. She was the misweighed scales of justice! He would set her straight.

The best detective stories begin with a damn good question. *I had a husband once. Who is he?* she asked. *I want you to find him and tell me about him.*

I think you would be in a much better position to do that, said Ersatz. *What would you like to know? Did he cheat on you, is he a gambler? Has his life failed without you? Is there another woman? Those are better, answerable, questions.*

No, she said. *All I want to know is what he is really like. Does he have a soul? What does he think about when he buttons his shirt, or brushes his teeth? I am lonely in my life, Mr. Ersatz. I do not work and spend a lot of time with myself and my thoughts.*

How do you know he is alive? Ersatz was careful to look at her straight, to show her he was on the level.

He is alive and he is an insurance adjustor and he works in an office tower downtown. He sends postcards. She had one of them with her. It was the city skyline at dawn. All it said was *Hello!* in a thin scrawl. *He sends one every year. They all say the same thing.*

Why did you leave him? said Ersatz, with piqued interest, staring at the *Hello!*

He left me. We fought constantly. We threw things at one another, we accused each other of indiscretions. After a while I questioned his moral and physical fibre. He became indignant. I said it was nothing to get indignant about. Then he left.

That sounds like straw, said Ersatz.

What? Her head turned. The heavy earring swung, and he thought of those women in cubist paintings. She was so close to the desk that Ersatz, if he stood, might have plucked the offending earring from its hole with the tip of his pen.

What breaks the camel's back, Ersatz said. *Not the true cause, just the final one.*

We had a stillborn child together. His name is Dreschl.

The ex-husband or the child?

Both.

That, said Ersatz, *sounds like a true starting point.* Ersatz was always miffed by people who expressed interest in the particulars of his career because they thought about spies or SWAT teams, both of which are not authentic private investigators. Or they thought about Sam Spade, who was too hard-boiled for Ersatz. Ersatz *wanted* to be Sam Spade, but the machismo was difficult to maintain. When he finally fell asleep, because sleeping was a struggle, his body relaxed. All the blunt and powerful traits he cultivated in daylight hours poured out of him as though he were only a vessel.

He explained to such people that a detective's job, at its root, is methodical and tedious. It is, he said, the assembling of facts, gathered from clues, into a narrative which results in a discovery. The real world was there for the eye to see, but it lacked something that needed to be found so people everywhere could sleep knowing the world was doing its damnedest to right itself. *The job,* he said, *is not much different from a physicist's or a mathematician's. Solve the problem or argument to receive empirical knowledge.* It was as simple as that. Although if it were so simple, Ersatz would sleep easily through the night.

Ersatz thought of this as he sat in the office later that evening and observed the few pieces of preliminary evidence the ex-wife had provided: a pile of photographs, two of the identical postcards, and a blue tee-shirt faded at the underarm seam and across the chest. *It is all I have of him,* she had said, *but I must entrust them to your concern.* The tee-shirt smelled androgynous and musty; it had been washed a thousand times. *It is the result of a marriage,* he thought. The postcards he had seen and tossed aside.

The pictures were the most interesting clue, a series depicting the same scene. Dreschl stood in the lobby of a business tower in a grey suit, arms at his sides, people milling about. Always it showed the back of his head. What was it he faced? It was an elevator. There were twenty photographs and each had a year dated on the back of the card, the earliest dated 1975, and in every picture there was a head and an elevator.

In some pictures Dreschl was alone and it was nearly impossible to discern the year from his suit. It was not the same grey suit in every photo, but they were of the same cut, from the same tailor, with the same measurements Dreschl had worn since his belly settled in its permanent place over the lip of his belt, probably not long before the 1975 date of the earliest photograph. The suit was bland but it was never out of style. Dreschl's hair was neat and pressed against his head. Those photographs in which Dreschl stood with strangers' company made it easier to identify each picture's proper chronological order; these people wore years like accessories in their haircuts, skirt lengths, the patterns of their prints. They blithely played a part in the world of each year. They rejoiced in their sentimental and temporary trends. *When ordinary people look at photographs of themselves*, thought Ersatz, *they blush and laugh at the passion and silliness with which they led their lives, the things to which they had pledged allegiance.* But as embarrassing as such moments are, they mark what was, what is, the passing of time. What has come, what may come again, and what cannot.

All of this is an example of typical detective work. From a series of crime scene photos one surveys and one conjectures. The closeness of the relationship between conjecture and the evidence of the survey is the measurement of success. But there were no hints to Dreschl's soul in these photographs, although there must be since the cliché is that pictures capture memory, and implicitly, the souls of people. There were other problems, too;

the origin of the photographs was also a mystery. Who had taken the photos of this man, in a single place, once a year for twenty years? Had the ex-wife neglected to mention they had been included with the postcards? They must've been.

Ersatz went to the office tower downtown where Dreschl's insurance company occupied the 13th floor. He sat in the lobby on a steel bench pressed against a large window opening into the intersection. It reminded him of reversible window shopping: look into the world and see the city available for a price. *Men and women of the street! Peer into the clean blue lobby of an office tower and see the souls of purgatory.* Ersatz crossed his legs and turned himself so he had the clearest view of the entire lobby.

Within moments there was the morning bottleneck. Streetcars dispersed coloured hordes through the revolving doors, and tags were shown to the deskman. The elevators chimed and rose. Men in blue suits held slightly tilted coffee cups while their superiors carried silver lidded travellers' mugs. Sunlight splashed on the marble floor through skylights of varying heights. Not anywhere was a sign of a man in a grey suit, but the photos implied Dreschl still worked here. The ex-wife had said so, too. Ersatz had not called the company for fear of tipping Dreschl off, but now he doubted himself and his target's reliability. To understand an animal you must observe it in its natural habitat, without the creature being self-conscious of its acknowledgment. Yet, where was Dreschl? Nowhere, he was nothing. Something had to be done.

Ersatz walked to the front desk. It was monitored by a black, bald man in a blue suit. He wheeled from side to side on a small chair, saying hello to the regulars, checking identification of the visitors, and typing into a computer.

My name is Plektos Ersatz. I am a private eye.

Yeah? My name is Alphonse Andolph. Can I help you?

Maybe, said Ersatz, sliding across a photograph. *I'm looking for this man. His name is Dreschl.*

Yeah. What about him? He cocked his head. *He is straining to remember,* thought Ersatz. Then Alphonse grinned.

Do you know where he is? said Ersatz.

Naw, said Alphonse. *See him in here in the mornings, yeah, but you never know when you're gonna see him. He's ordinary, man, but you recognize him. He is the most conspicuous ordinary man in the world. But he's regular. I mean, you don't always see him right first-thing in the morning. Sometimes he comes in nine-thirty, ten o'clock.*

I have a picture, said Ersatz.

Yeah? said Alphonse.

Ersatz waited for Alphonse to continue. When he didn't, Ersatz pointed at the picture of Dreschl waiting for the elevator. *Does this mean anything to you?*

Alphonse shook his head. *That's when he's alone, everyone up in the tower working by then. He leaves everyday at five minutes to five. And he keeps coming, I mean he's still working here, so he must be some kind of punctual, even if he's always late in the morning.*

So something makes him late, said Ersatz.

Yeah, maybe. How should I know? I don't got time for it. Alphonse was growing impatient.

Ersatz said: *What about the computer—do you have any records of him in there? All I know of this man is that he works here. There is little else to go on.*

Then, sir, you got to go through proper channels. You're a private eye, aren't you? I've spent every day of my working-life at this desk. Every year the database of visitors and employees gets bigger and the computer gets smaller.

I understand, said Ersatz, who did not.

Alphonse nodded as though he had dispensed sage wisdom. Then he looked down his nose at Ersatz, but he smiled, emphasizing his point through two emotions. *Now we both have occupations to be occupyin' our time with,*

Mr. Ersatz. Ersatz knew this was a euphemism for good-bye.

Ersatz spent the entire day sitting on the bench, blending into the city. At lunch he bought a panini from an Italian deli across the street. He mulled over the things he knew about Dreschl, but since he knew little it was more dreaming than serious thinking. He had to be patient.

Then at five-to-five, good to Alphonse's word, he saw a grey suit. He followed it to the parking lot and to a purple car. The car pulled out of the space. Ersatz ran up a set of dirty stairs to the street and hailed a cab. He followed the car for several blocks, shouting directions. The cab driver was puzzled as the purple car made many right-hand turns at random intervals; several times they crossed streets they had already travelled on. Eventually the cab driver lost the purple car. *Sorry*, said the driver with a tip of his hat. *No, that is perfectly alright,* said Ersatz, and he paid the fare. Then he thought: *He must have known he was being followed.*

But that was not the case. For Ersatz attempted to follow Dreschl somewhere, *anywhere,* for the next week, in cabs or his own car. Everything about Dreschl's exit was purposeful and exact and absolutely predictable. However, even if he waited in his car at the foot of the parking garage, he would be eluded be another random series of turns. Ersatz dressed in disguises to throw off his target, but always the car drove calmy away and into the city, where it dissolved. *He does not know he is being followed,* said Ersatz. *He is driving around like an idiot.*

He tried to telephone the ex-wife but there was never an answer, so he billed her for the mounting expenses he racked up and assumed she would contact him if she had a complaint. Ersatz sat at his desk, in his pajamas, with the pictures. The comfort and looseness helped him think. This was an unusual case but the goal was large and broad: it was not to find a missing earring that might unlock a matricidal murder case, it was not a search for buried treasure. It was much simpler, and he had clues: nearly identical photographs, identical postcards, and a tee-shirt. He had only to prove Dreschl's existence, capture some evidence of it, maybe. And if the ex-wife desired so (or maybe if she didn't, if it was only to satisfy Ersatz's curiosity) he might glimpse and reason with the man's soul, discover his *motive.* But the entire task, which should have been simple, was proving itself otherwise.

Dreschl was a predictable man. As an insurance adjustor he knew exactly how much time he would spend in his lifetime doing boring and necessary tasks, like eating or sleeping or waiting for the elevator. It must have been his hobby too, his obsession. Percentages and risks were his occupation, but everyone understands and calculates risk and chance in their daily activities. *It is the nature of what we do*, Ersatz thought. *I have taken a dozen risks to find this man, and every single one has failed.* Yet Dreschl's life was immaculately planned; it simply ran according to a pattern Ersatz couldn't detect. No man randomly drives his car, or maintains a job without any punctuality. Dreschl was a pattern, he must have been, but Ersatz failed to see it, and a private investigator unable to detect patterns is a failure.

He no longer slept at all during night. The moon was thin as a nail clipping, casting no light upon his face. But still he was awake. *Good lord, I have lost faith in myself. I am not at all hard-boiled.*

In the morning he talked to Alphonse. *Do you have any idea where Dreschl goes?*

At five o'clock I take off my uniform and go home. I forget about what happened here.

Ersatz leaned over the counter, whispered: *Dreschl leaves at five-to-five. So you are still an employee when he leaves. You can help me. You can say goodnight to him. Tell him to have a pleasant evening. Ask if he has plans. Anything, Mr. Alphonse Andolph. The case, it's going nowhere. I need a sting.*

Alphonse bristled. His eyebrows rounded into half-moons and he pursed his lips. *Mr. Ersatz, I operate my business on a code of ethics. It is in my job description. Violate at your own risk, and you shall become a jobless wanderer. You cannot force my enlistment, sir.*

Ersatz was speechless. He shook Alphonse's hand. *Yes,* he said, *we both have occupations to be occupying ourselves.*

Looking back on his latest conversation with Alphonse, Ersatz knew he had lost his composure. He was no longer the image of a detective to Mr. Andolph but a curious and obsessive character. How close might Alphonse's finger have been to the security button throughout their conversation? Perhaps dangerously close. If he had been escorted out between the burly arms of men wearing identical blue uniforms he would have retreated to the worst possible end of his occupational spectrum: he would be a *perp.* Ersatz was too distraught to work. He went home well before four o'clock, admitting his defeat by doing nothing.

He telephoned the ex-wife to ask for advice under the guise of professional questions. Surely there was more she knew and yet to tell him. He tried several times throughout the night, and at first there was no answer. He tried again when he could not sleep, and at last she picked up the phone.

I thought something was terribly wrong, she said, *for you to call now.*

Ersatz explained that he had called earlier but she shrugged off his inquiries. No, she did not know what else to tell him. In all honesty her memories of the former spouse had gone hazy. She said nothing about the expense bills. He wished her a good night and hung up the phone. At least she hadn't asked him how the search was going, if he had any answers. This is what he thought, lying on top his comforter and wiggling his toes in the cool darkness until the sun peeked in.

Ersatz knew that complex rules govern behaviour. Broad social systems, notions of morality, and truth and justice. These were large and abstract and encompassed everyone in the city, in the country even: in a utopia, it would involve the entire world. More specifically there were codes of conduct set in legal type arranged by occupation. Hippocratic oaths and other such documents and pledges. And then, on the most intimate level of human interaction, there were common manners, human decency. How fragile they all seemed, yet how inviolable! Alphonse Andolph *had* given him sage wisdom.

This is what he was thinking of as he broke all these fragile and inviolable laws and slashed two of Dreschl's tires with a knife one morning before he went to lunch. He shoved the knife back in his pocket. It was a perfect plan; the predictable and organized man would have to do something unique. *It is the unique things we do that make us interesting!* Ersatz thought. *Then I may at least follow the man where he goes, and perhaps, if fortune is prepared, learn an insight about the man!*

Ersatz ate lunch at the deli again. They made a delicious corned beef on rye with a large dill pickle. It brought his senses alive and he ordered a pop. He would be ready to discover this evening, with his senses at this height; enlightenment was near. He put the second half of the sandwich into the tote bag carrying his few pieces of evidence: the tee-shirt and photographs. He walked back to the lobby and prepared to wait. When he walked in the door he saw Alphonse and nodded.

Sir Ersatz, Alphonse said, rising from his chair and approaching the detective: *May I see your pockets and tote bag?*

Stunned by a question he hadn't expected, although a detective should always expect the unexpected, Ersatz flustered: *No. It is my private business. Besides, you have no reason. Why do you wish to see my bag?*

As good a reason, sir, as you have for following that fellow from the insurance agency.

Yes, and you were no help to me then, either. So why should I help you now? That is the world, full of people who want help but refuse to give it.

True, said Alphonse, *but that man is accused of no crime but of being himself.* He slid across the desk to Ersatz a security photograph of the detective slashing Dreschl's tires. He leaned over as though to inspect the photograph alongside Ersatz, to describe it to him as Ersatz had once described a picture to him. He was leaning in very close, his elbows propped on the counter. Ersatz could smell his breath. It smelled like chicken and mayonnaise. Alphonse Andolph had pressed the security button!

No! Ersatz shouted, and he did what any perp would do: he ran as fast as he could and hoped it was fast enough to run off the earth. He knew Alphonse would not follow him. The man was chained to that desk until five o'clock. But there were others: three large men in uniforms chased him through the lobby. Ersatz ran into a stairwell and down to the basement. It was the only route he knew, so he ran it. He pushed out into the garage and ran past tracks of cars. The tote bag thumped against his lower back and buttocks, a constant reminder: *Dreschl, Dreschl is the cause of all this!* He ran up the sloped floor toward the toll booth and impending daylight. *Stop!* shouted the men. *Stop!* But Ersatz did not. He refused to be a criminal. *I am a detective!* he shouted, but it sounded more like heavy wheezing.

The men were gaining. Ersatz shrugged off the tote bag and threw it behind a row of cars as he turned the corner and faced another slope. He broke through the tollgate like a sprinter. Sprinting! There was a career he had not thought of before now. He was in the sunlight and free. He ducked into the crowds of shoppers and businessmen. He had escaped, like a genuine criminal. When he stopped to take a breath he hardly recognized himself. The breaths did not come easier with rest. The breathlessness of running stuck with him. *Ah, that is guilt, that is failure,* he said.

At first Ersatz did not dare return to the office tower. Surely Dreschl had been informed. The animal, the object of study, was alerted to the intruder and his actions could no longer be trusted as authentic. And that was all there was to begin with. He had only been asked to follow a man and learn something about him. Now what could he know? Only the roles he himself played, right and wrong.

Had he a chance of getting back in the lobby? Only if Alphonse Andolph was not present. But Alphonse had manned the desk every day Ersatz kept watch for

Dreschl. He must have sick days; he is only a man and susceptible to viruses, to illness, to death. He only had to go to the lobby every day, secretly, until one day when he would discover that Alphonse was not there. It would happen. Gamblers say if you have a one in two hundred million chance of winning the lottery then you will eventually win it at some point, if you had all eternity to do so: maybe it would take all two hundred million chances, maybe even more, but it is achievable. *No,* thought Ersatz, *that is optimism and that is not true. There is an equal chance one will never win. That if you flip a coin there is a one in two chance your call is right. If you pick a side and stick with it, it is only a matter of time before its surface appears. But that is not true at all. The coin may never flip the way one wishes.*

For days he sat at home thinking about Dreschl, letting the man fill his mind. He waited to be interrupted by the angry client, dissatisfied and seeking the money she had wasted on Ersatz's services. But she never called. She must have had a life of her own to contend with. So he thought about Dreschl and crafted his story.

What was Dreschl life's like? What are the constants of life, what are its changes? He hated himself for his vague questions. The constant which had set the whole awful affair into motion: it was the child. The ex-wife

had been provoked by the child, and he was in turn provoked by her. It was all motivated by the child. Children, alive or dead, motivate men and women. Risk and
death, yes, they lead to careers in insurance. But Dreschl
—was Dreschl motivated by the child? Plektos Ersatz's
imagination was vivid; in it Dreschl was alive and filled
with soul. He must! Yet Ersatz had not seen it, the man's
affectation for the lost child, which certainly affects men
and women profoundly! He felt very in tune with his
subject. He thought and the man in his mind moved.
He felt Ersatz's grief, raised his arm when Ersatz raised
his. They laughed together. *The man I preyed upon is my
only companion*, thought Ersatz. Yet it was all conjecture.
It was a sad story and he allowed himself to believe it. A
blind, ridiculous faith that seeped and evaporated as
quickly as body heat.

So he went back to the parking garage to find his
evidence, conjecture's real world relation. He saw
Dreschl's car and was elated. Yes, the purple car was there,
in the rows of silver and purple and red and black cars.
He stood a moment with his hands clasped behind his
head, his thumbs lightly massaging his neck. *Yes!* Then
he turned and retraced the steps of his escape. He had
turned and thrown the bag somewhere. It was here!
Might it still be here?

It was, only a few cars removed from Dreschl's own. He picked it up and peered inside. The photographs were still there. Good, good. But the tee-shirt was gone. Someone had taken the shirt! He groaned. But he had what he had. And although he knew Dreschl was not far away he knew Alphonse Andolph was there too. Where Alphonse Andolph patrolled, Ersatz was not welcome.

Ersatz went home and stared at the photographs. He could tell the year from the elevator doors, he realized, if he looked hard enough. If not the exact year at least the progression of years, as the elevator doors faded and were changed, or the buttons replaced. Yes, but what good was it? Why had he gone back for the evidence?

Perhaps sensing his despondency, the ex-wife called. *You're fired,* she said. *I've paid you five thousand dollars for nothing. I've been waiting. Where is the payoff? You haven't got one! You're a middling detective. You're relieved of your duties. Never mind the money. Just go away.*

Like a certain husband! Ersatz retorted. *Tell them to pack up and go away when their soul is of no more use to you, regardless of how you have destroyed them!*

You're no human being, she shouted, and hung up.

But Ersatz was not finished. Tears dripped off his face and onto his white tee-shirt and pajamas. What detective doesn't wear a suit himself? Only a failure. *I do not want* to be a detective any longer, it is good that I am not! he shouted. *I only want to be a witness! To see it all before me at once, the conjecture and the real world. I do not have the strength to put the story together! My eyes lie, my mind is feeble. I am without occupation. There is no saving me!* And he cried, the sobs moistening his tee-shirt, visibly marking his sorrow.

Dreschl's tee-shirt! Yes, it too bore stain markings. It was the blanket in which the child had been wrapped! Yes, but it had been washed a thousand times. Yes, Dreschl had cried into the shirt. And then, then what? There is a child in his hands, the cranium malformed, hardly the size of tennis ball, and softer. The body limp, the neck tenuously attached to a mottled body of red and white. Does Dreschl feel sadness? He must! Dreschl assesses risks and damages. *What else might I say about Dreschl?* He is not perfidious but he is generally predictable! Yes, with the baby in his arms what is predictable, what is next? Dreschl wraps the child in the tee-shirt. Yes!

Ersatz was ecstatic. A breakthrough! He bypassed the telephone and went to the ex-wife's house to see her face.

What is wrong now, she said crossly through the wood door, without bothering to ask who it was. The door, heavy and dense, opened slowly. She was dressed as she had been in Ersatz's office. Oh, the office! How long since he had been there, comfortable and secure!

This case has nothing to do with your husband, boomed Ersatz with authority, wearing his pajamas. *It has everything to do with your child!*

What? shouted the wife.

The shirt belonged to the child! The child is alive!

That is not true! She wore matched earrings and her head was nearly unrecognizable, so straight and level and cunning it was upon her neck, without that insouciant tilt! It had led him astray. Yes, the scales of justice were even! He had detected, he had made his bold conjecture. On clues, without ever talking with a man. Never mind Alphonse Andolph, he was no help. Ersatz had made a discovery of a soul without seeing another man's soul; he felt alive in another man.

Dreschl did not dispose of the child! He gave the child to the world, in his shirt! You gave birth somewhere, I don't know where and it hardly matters to me, and Dreschl took the child. He was already dead, you said to me, but he was not. Put him somewhere, anywhere, but take him away from me. I do not wish to see him. Dreschl refused. You threatened, and he acquiesced under your omnipresent rage. Dreschl does something with the child: he leaves you. But the shirt stays. What did Dreschl do with the child? You do not know! So you come to me. Tell me the soul of my husband you say, as though it were only curiosity. But really you are asking me: What makes a man compassionate? What makes a man feel, what makes a man of no risk take one?

Her face looked as though it would implode from the barometric pressure of her anger. All the features of her face pulled together in a tight cave around her nose. *You have not a shred of proof, of anything suggesting that you are to be believed! Five thousand dollars for stories, for rubbish! So you seek a child instead of a man, so what?* she said. *I gave you a job and you failed. Whatever I think, whatever it is I look for, all the business it is of yours is to find anything. Yet all you have done is craft a ridiculous story. It will not stand up in a court of law. It will not even stand a test of manners among civil people pretending to be interested. You have no child, you have no Dreschl! It is only a theory and theories do not work in most occupations. You are not to be believed. It's only an implausible tale.*

But it touches my heart! shouted Ersatz. *That is enough to make me believe it. I have conjectured with my own mind. It is as close as I may come! It is what you have asked!*

Then, surprising him, the ex-wife sat down on the steps and wept. He was not a detective, no. Detectives should feel no emotion but success or failure. He wanted to comfort her but she would not let him.

A sad story of Dreschl, and I had believed it, thought Ersatz. *But what of it was true?* Ersatz did not know. The wife stood up and went inside, closing the door so Ersatz could not see her. He had studied the details of Dreschl's story, eager for the root. *But where is the root in people's souls*, thought Ersatz as the moon radiated, *at what point does one say 'Yes, there is the obvious cause, what eludes us, what might make our souls whole?'*

AFTER THE
DOCTOR DIED IN
HIS NOVEL

The good doctor, who resembled Charles Bovary, died upon discovering his missing wife's body upholstered in his favourite Victorian armchair. The body had been dissected and hidden in the chair, which was hastily sewn again. When the doctor sat, the chair cracked under his weight. The stitching on the bottom of the chair tore apart. A once-lovely hand fell and landed next to the doctor's foot. The doctor bent over to see what had fallen. Then he died.

The first draft's death was by shock or a sudden heart attack. In the second draft, the author considered the doctor's vengeful, redemptive suicide, so he might be reunited with his murdered wife. The author did not know what to do and he led the good doctor on in agony while the particulars of his fate were decided. He puzzled over the good doctor while in the back of the doctor's mind (which was likely further back in the author's own mind) the author's fate was also decided vis-à-vis the million decisions a human brain makes in the instance a typewriter imprints a letter. He made no further resolutions, but to the doctor's horror, pronounced the doctor dead of *something*.

The author went outside for a cigarette in the daylight and sat in a porch chair. He had not been very good to the doctor or the book. The plot was threadbare and horribly orthodox. The doctor was indecisive and could not tell the author the slightest detail of how his life should be lived; he knew (both the author and the doctor) his most basic pleasures but not his greatest yearnings. That was the problem: the novel was not about great yearnings. The author snuffed out his cigarette and walked back to his writing desk in the book-lined room.

The author was sixty-eight and his fingers were thin and tired. So he typed furiously, since he knew his own time, like the good doctor's, was waning and could in a moment be slammed into the darkness. The author wrote long past the good doctor's death, but he could not put the doctor out of his mind.

You! shouted the doctor at the author, *Who killed my wife? I need to know who killed my wife before I die.*

The author replied that he didn't know yet, this was a mystery novel in progress. This was a partial truth. The author had in fact written an entire draft of the book down to the epilogue, but he had left the slightest margin for debating the murderer's identity. He knew this was probably sloppy writing and that he should be much more authoritative. But the author now felt closer to sixty-nine than sixty-eight and thought *I'll probably be dead before the reviews come in, so what is the use in caring.* He was nevertheless touched by the good doctor's concern, a quality the author did not know he had.

In the text's death scene, the doctor lay on the floor of his book-lined study, which was based, rather transparently, on the author's own study. Piles of reference books were on the floor and classic paperbacks held the highest shelves. The doctor wrapped himself around the legs of the desk and sobbed to himself.

Tell me, please!

The author shrugged. *I'm sorry, good doctor, but there's room for controversy. I simply don't know who is to blame. It was me,* he added, *just blame me for her death, if it will make it palatable for you.*

It's no use, wailed the doctor. *You're no more responsible for her death than you are for your own.*

The author was perplexed. He was quite used to being the cause of his characters' deaths, it happened frequently. *What do you mean?* he asked.

I mean, said the good doctor, *that you will die as surely as I will, you'll die and my wife again, for eternity when you die,* and he stopped amidst a stream of tears. *I mean that my wife is dead and I am dead, and when you die I'll be dead again for good and her the same, and when your son dies you'll be dead again but for good, and your father doubly dead, your grandfather triply. You're not responsible, you can't help it, but you've killed so many people and have no idea that you are to blame.*

The author did not understand what the doctor was saying, but he said it with such passion, he felt moved. He suddenly hated his book, all of his books, and felt terrible he caused such pain to more people than he knew. With his own impending death, the author did not want to be guilty. He walked to the bookshelf and searched for copies of his books. He wanted to erase the names, or blot them out with a magic marker, or slam their covers and kill those characters far better than he had killed the good doctor, who refused to leave him alone. Part of him knew his own foolishness but he pulled books off the shelves and dropped them on his feet and on each other. He found his own book and threw it on the desk. *One!* He found another. *Two!* In his ardour he nearly toppled a bookshelf, but steadied it at the last moment. The books, however, rained on him:

reference texts thumped his forehead. He fell, cracking his skull on the corner of his heavy desk. As he lay dying, he tried to ascertain the cause of his death. Was it a heart attack, or a severe brain injury? He died, like many people, before he knew the cause.

The author's body was discovered by his next-door neighbour, a kindly pediatrician who worried when he did not see the author talking to himself on his porch in the morning. The author was not unfriendly although, perhaps, disillusioned. Even so the pediatrician had great respect for the author's work. He saw much of himself in the characters, much he could *relate to*. That was the phrase used in his book club, and he was very sad that he would tell them that the good author next door, whom they had all read after studying Flaubert, had passed on. There was nothing he could have done to help. He lowered the good author's eyelids and arranged the fallen books into neat piles on the floor. Then he lifted the author's heavy body to the carpet, where it seemed more dignified and at peace. He called an ambulance and, while he waited, read fragments of the good author's unfinished mystery manuscript, which he found sloppy and unrefined.

THE ELEVATOR

Although only one of many indignations, Saul was tired of being called a young Jewish boy by his boss Plouffe and told him that the Marwell Advertising Agency (the world's third largest) could go fuck itself and as many Jewish boys as Mr. Plouffe's cock could handle. Plouffe, who was graceful despite his immense obesity, wiped a sweaty palm across his brow and told Saul without a hint of reproach that he understood; the boy had suffered many indignations, not the least of which was being born Jewish. By nature Saul was very apologetic. He had great green eyes which begged out for approval, and he didn't want to leave his young, pregnant wife worrying about his impetuousness. He gave Plouffe two weeks' notice and went back to working copy.

On his last Friday, Saul arrived at the office in a fine shirt and red silk tie. He was finishing his final piece of copy for the Marwell Advertising Agency and feeling sublimely happy when an anxious temp burst into the office shrieking:

One of the elevators in the East Wing plummeted several floors and killed four people inside!

The proofers, the designers, and the executives were understandably alarmed and saddened by the event, although it was quite unlikely that any of them knew of the victims, but they knew that their own week was over and that it could have been any number of them in that particular elevator, hurriedly leaving the tower to take full advantage of the weekend. Twenty minutes later Saul was in Mr. Plouffe's office.

Oh no, said Mr. Plouffe. *It is such terrible news to give to you Saul, but we did lose people in the tragedy. Two fantastic copy editors—Flagellan and McElroy. They were good men, very good workers. They will be missed. You will be missed. What an unfortunate thing to have happen on your last day, that it should taint your memories of the Marwell Advertising Agency.*

The last indignity Saul wanted to endure was the humiliation of willfully leaving a job from which Flagellan and McElroy had been forcibly deprived. He did not want to tell his young wife that he successfully exited the building at four-thirty in the sunlit afternoon while hordes of emergency service personnel bagged the unfortunately deceased in an elevator in the nearby East Wing.

I would be happy, Saul said, *to come in on Monday. I will finish their last projects for them. It is, I think, what is right. Besides, my wife and I could certainly use a few more dollars.*

You are a good man, and prudent, said Mr. Plouffe. *You remind me of myself.*

He dismissed Saul with a faint smile and a shrug of his fat heavy hand. Saul took off his silk tie, bundled it into a soft ball and put it in his pocket before walking down sixty-five flights of stairs. Saul arrived home late, his chicken dinner cold on the table, his wife asleep on the futon in the living room. Her tiny bulge rocked itself to sleep under her laboured breathing.

On Monday morning the mood at Marwell was grim exhaustion. Saul was a half-hour late for Flagellan and McElroy's shifts. The previous Friday evening the building had been half empty. Everyone in the high-rise had begun their shift at eight o'clock, so bottlenecks formed in the stairwells: people were jostled and unkind words were tossed. The most fit and able-bodied walkers were forced to slow their pace to trod behind the slower employees. Saul brushed beads of sweat off his face as he walked.

The entire week was a trudge, and on Friday Saul was glad to be leaving the Marwell Agency for the second time. He again gathered his things, stepped into Mr. Plouffe's office and shook his fat hand.

Actually, said Mr. Plouffe, leaning on the desktop, *we had a little accident in the stairwell. Someone broke a heel, and fell backward into a crowd on the forty-fifth floor. We lost a few more good people, but, thankfully, only to mild charley horses and knee sprains. Can you fill-in next week as well? I'll give you time-and-a-half. Needless to say,* he added, *heels are hitherto banned in this office building.*

The baby in his wife's stomach was getting bigger and his wife was eating plenty of food and making preparations for a nursery. It was prescient to accept. He walked back to his cubicle, unpacked his things, and passed several barefoot women on the staircase who walked carefully so as not to step on each other's toes. When he arrived home there was no dinner on the table. His wife had fallen asleep in the bathtub. He drained the water and laid her on the bed, waiting for the cold air to gently wake her.

Next Monday all employees wore hard-soled walking shoes. Climbing the staircases was less daunting: people moved faster and with confidence, but the racket raised by the pounding shoes was deafening. Saul arrived at his desk more promptly than the week before but with headaches. He could not focus on the work before him. Plouffe called Saul into his office for a chat, and Saul was miffed that Mr. Plouffe, who had been so acquiescent when Saul called him a Jew-cock gobbler weeks earlier, was now disenchanted with Saul's youthful good spirit of willingness. By Friday the aggravation of Mr. Plouffe's consternation and the pounding of shoes proved too much. That morning he again put on his finest shirt and jacket. That afternoon he saw Plouffe, who understood, as he had heard this before. Saul was enraged by his boss's quiet acceptance and faint, dimpled smile as he handed Saul his last paycheque.

We are sorry to have you leave us again, Saul. Your future was very bright here.

Saul packed his plant, the pictures of his wife and the ultrasound of his child, his motivational poster, and his copy of *The Thirteen Habits of Highly Effective People* in a flimsy cardboard box and, without thought, caught the elevator. The trials of the stairwells had caused many people to reconsider their fear, and by the time the elevator reached the fiftieth floor it was packed with long faces and weary mouths, employees dressed in perky ensembles. Somewhere near the twentieth floor the elevator stopped and the power was cut. Even the tiny red emergency bulb was out. The dark made the keen smell of body odour and make-up more pervasive. In the light the employees mumbled to people they knew, but in the dark it did not matter who you were or worked for. They stood shoulder to shoulder and could do little more than turn their heads, but, since it was dark, they did not bother with even that. They gurgled and mumbled that they were going to miss the convenient trains. Some had to use the facilities.

Saul felt claustrophobic and he tried not to claw for air. He clutched the brown box to his chest, attempting not to thump it against the person in front of him. After five minutes a voice came over a loudspeaker announcing that help was forthcoming. Fifteen minutes later the power was still out. Saul imagined that things were happening around him he could not see; he was convinced two men to his left were groping each other's genitals, and that the man in front of him had dropped his pants. Then he felt his box being jostled. He was sure people were taking his belongings and stuffing them in their jackets or briefcases or down their pants. The box felt increasingly light. Since he held it tightly from the bottom he could do little and dared not accuse the figures of thievery. Saul felt his wallet being lifted from his back pocket and the arms of the people beside him shuffling and moving about: passing around, no doubt, his severance pay and cheque. He was still Jewish. He was poor. His wife was probably already asleep with the baby.

When the elevator resumed and chimed the bottom floor Saul unbundled his wrinkled tie and walked outside with his empty box.

ONE TRICK PONY

Barb Moody's single talent was juggling, and as far as she was concerned, it would be her life's work. It was a talent everyone, including her parents, admitted she had. So although she was only ten, however precocious, no one stopped her when she carried a duffel bag and three blue balls to the town square on the first Saturday of April and began to juggle. That night her parents prepared a roast and poured an extra glass of grapefruit juice, figuring Barb's pursuit was a childhood dalliance. But Barb did not come home. Her father found her room cold and Barb-less in the early morning. The cold made him tie his robe tight and he suspected he was not so happy that his daughter had found her life's calling.

He went to the top of Bowflight Hill, overlooking the town centre, and saw cars circling the square and pulling out of donut shops and weekend restaurants. And in the centre, a tiny parkette filled with goose shit, he saw three balls rhythmically flicking in the darkness. He sat on the grass until the wet seeped through his robe and then he walked home, surprised to find his wife still asleep. He made breakfast for one and ate it watching a television program on migratory birds.

On Monday Barb did not attend class. The principal called her father, who explained Barb had found her life's work. The principal prickled, but did not say: *She's a ten-year-old girl. You left her alone in the square?* It was the school's policy to promote its students' life goals and dreams, however tiny or premature. *If Barb Moody has the gumbo to set out and achieve her goal at ten years of life,* he thought, *she deserves to be treated as an adult.* All the children put pictures of themselves up in the halls, dressed as astronauts and journalists and hockey players (one boy had aspirations toward being a stripper) and all of them were taken seriously. The children were commended for their foresight and ambition, and the teachers told them their dreams were unequivocally attainable. The principal was young and he figured it would be many years before he might note the positive effect he had on children. Barb Moody was actually an intense pleasure, having peaked so young. So he wrote a note to Barb Moody's teacher saying that Barb Moody was on indefinite leave in pursuit of extracurricular talents.

The teachers thought this was all wonderful news, and they told their students. The students were amazed and many went to the park. The children hooted and cheered until they were bored, and went home to their families.

Barb continued to juggle through that first week. Papers published photographs of the girl-wonder; the mayor asked her questions and publicly praised her resolve. *The Guinness Book of World Records* was consulted. Fellow jugglers came in small droves and juggled with Barb, who came to be known as the Amazing Girl Juggler. During these days Barb's father and mother were very popular people, and Barb's father watched his wife run from her matronly persona. She abandoned the PTA to share drinks with the mayor, who had plenty of flattering things to say about her and her daughter, and she attended parties as the guest of honour. At night she never came home, and Barb's father slept alone. She was glad to be free of the duty of washing Barb's clothes and cooking her food. Barb's father knew this was not because she was a terrible woman, but because she was born to be a socialite, not a mother. He grew tired of the absurd praise he received for doing nothing at all to stop his daughter, which he now suspected was not right at all, and he avoided the public by spending his days in Barb's bedroom.

The hoopla would stop. Within days the students forgot Barb Moody. The teachers forgot her too: Barb

Moody's desk was filled by a foreign-exchange student from Beijing. It was as if he'd always sat in that spot, and it was as if Barb Moody had never been. The principal also forgot Barb Moody, though he recalled he had once had a student so intent on delinquency she had dropped out of elementary school. But he could not remember the name, and assured himself that any student dumb enough to drop out of school was someone not worth remembering, except Einstein, who was a very peculiar exception. So it became that Barb Moody was left alone in the square, except for the company of a few pigeons, juggling in the rising and falling sunlight of each day.

The life plan Barb's father had set for himself evaporated overnight. Since his daughter was out of the house and there was no college debt to repay, he figured it was time to retire from his construction job. He spent a day or two mulling around the house, cutting the grass and putting in a new privacy fence to keep out the eyes of his neighbours, but it all happened much too fast for his liking. He could not focus. He was bored and growing old much too quickly. His wife had gone and he could not call his work buddies. They were all toiling to pay mortgages, for their children's extracurricular sports and mounting expenses. They were envious of Barb's father and when he telephoned, they were curt, and they hung up without saying goodbye. He was denied access to seniors' clubs and denied discounts on food on account that he was not nearly old enough. He argued that he *was* in his golden years, but the cashiers all told him that didn't matter, then smiled and congratulated him on his daughter's success. *What a fine girl,* they said, *ten years old and the dolls completely forgotten! If only she had chosen medical school or some such profession, imagine what she might accomplish! But, you're right, she looks happy—and what more could a father ask?* He always nodded quickly (yes, a father could ask for nothing more) and left the supermarket near tears. He was tired of people and thought about buying a very large television, the gift he had promised himself when he retired. But his pension was too small. Instead, he bought used romance novels and contemplated his old life while eating soup purchased at full price.

Her father thought the juggling would cease when Barb was hungry enough to return home; at the very least (and to him this sounded unbearably cruel) she would crawl home after collapsing of malnutrition, the balls rolling into the gutters at her feet. Or before then, if someone convinced the police that she had to be brought home, that she was, in some way, a civic nuisance. He wondered if her idle activity might be considered so. Then he could perhaps come out of retirement. He felt his life was progressing too quickly: he was only thirty-eight, yet he was in his golden years. By the time he was fifty he would be very bored. He thought he and his wife could perhaps have more children, but he worried they might be equally un-usual. Besides, his wife was gone and he contented him-self by making love to a sock while staring at a soft-core magazine. She was free from the PTA meetings and living the wild life of a young debutante. She was likely having sex with a very young man, and each time he came into the sock, a vision came upon him: there he was, a gangly geriatric, a sock slipping from his limp member.

He went to the parkette to talk to his daughter. Her hair was greasy and tangled. She had snot all over her clothes, which had dirtied to the colour of mustard. She was thin but she looked happy.

Hi, Father, she said.

Hi, honey.

Don't come too close, you'll hit my balls.

Don't you think you might like to come home, Barb? Your mom and I, we miss you very much, we hardly know what to do without you. Since you left the house, I've retired.

It felt like the thing to do at the time, you know, since we had finished, I suppose, raising you. Won't you reconsider?

I'm sorry, Father, but I can't. This is what I want to do.

It pained him terribly to hear his daughter sound so old. She had never called him Father before. He was very confused.

Have we finished raising you?

I suppose so, she said. *I'm doing what I'm going to be doing the rest of my life.*

You don't know everything you need to know, he insisted. *Come home. You don't know anything about math, or finding an apartment. Sex, we haven't had the sex conversation yet. What do you know?*

Nothing, Father, but I don't need to. I won't be having sex, or solving math equations, or finding an apartment. I'm juggling.

He went home, leaving Barb to toss the balls as the morning traffic belched exhaust into the square. He was very afraid for his daughter and he contemplated dragging her back home. He called Child Services, who made it very clear that kidnapping was bad parenting. If they caught him disrupting his daughter's dreams she would be placed in foster-care where she could juggle for as long as she wished. Barb's father was desperate for things to return to normal. He called a pediatrician and asked him how long Barb could live without eating. He said *a couple of weeks, maybe a little longer, but it is impossible to tell.* No child had ever starved themselves intentionally while juggling; there were no statistics or research that might prove useful. *But,* he assured, if it can be called assurance, *if she has been doing this for more than two weeks, and she has not stopped to eat, as you say, she may collapse at any moment.* He lowered his voice, then added: *Once she's unconscious, unable to make a decision for herself, she will be your responsibility again. She will be your duty and your right, and I will have no choice but to oblige your wishes.*

The doctor's advice sounded very good.

For the next few mornings, sitting cross-legged on a blanket, he watched her juggle from the top of the hill. Fear clutched at him. The arc of the balls seemed to grow smaller by the day. Barb was weakening. Her father felt a terrible confluence of emotions: he was happy she was driven, so happy she was happy, and yet he yearned to have her come home and return the shambles of his life to normal, to bring back his wayward wife. He went home and grabbed three large grapefruits from the fridge. They were the only similarly circular objects in the house. He went outside with the grapefruits and practiced juggling them. He was terrible and never made it past two or three cycles. Two or three cycles was enough.

At eight the next morning he went to the parkette with his grapefruit. Barb was sitting on the grass, juggling. She stunk and dark circles of dirt hooded her eyelids. Barb's father was terrified that both her life and his old life were receding before his eyes. He tried to juggle.

Look, honey!

He dropped a grapefruit and she laughed. He tried again and failed. It didn't feel bad to be bested by his daughter of ten years. They laughed and he threw his grapefruit. He stole glances at Barb and secretly hoped she would collapse soon.

She lasted four more days, and her father never left her side, though the juggling infuriated him. He never seemed to get better and the five days seemed like five years. She finally collapsed, and her father felt not fear, but elation, as each of the balls fell on top of her body and rolled off her overalls into the street, where they were crushed by traffic. He slung her over her shoulder and took her to the hospital.

She was breathing when they arrived at the hospital's silver revolving doors. Barb's father waited for the doctor outside the emergency room until Dr. Brown, tall and pale, strode purposefully to meet him.

I'm very sorry, he said, *but Barb has specifically asked not to be resuscitated.*

What? said Barb's father.

It's all right here, he said.

He held a tiny yellow note folded into four squares. Inside was his daughter's blocky handwriting.

She must have prepared it before she began working, said Dr. Brown. *It specifically requests that she be left to die. I found it in her pocket.*

That's ridiculous! shouted Barb's father. *I'm her father! She's ten. Ten fucking years old! She drinks juice, she's in the sixth grade!*

She has lived the final weeks of her life as an independent, said Dr. Brown. *She had her own occupation. She was emancipated from your house. She was a dropout. She has every right to decide her life.*

Satisfied, the doctor turned away.

The note! shouted Barb's father. But the doctor had already crumpled it in his pocket.

THE DEPORTEE

Polk and his son Micah lived in a green neighbourhood uptown. They had lived there for ten years, since Micah was born and his mother died. It was not a rash decision to move even then because Polk knew the city very well, and wanted to find somewhere quiet and free of memories in which to raise his son. It was safe, and people walked their dogs or mowed their lawns. Once, children even played, laughing, in the gush of a busted hydrant like they were in the Bronx.

Polk was lonely on those first nights when Micah's cries rang off the empty walls, but those days of mourning were short-lived. Once Micah began to crawl Polk's mind was entirely preoccupied with his son. Polk took a 'desk job' and was delighted he had to tell his neighbours no more than that when he was asked—everyone seemed to know what he meant, or they had lost interest—and he kept his home sparsely decorated, not as a reminder of the home's impermanence but to limit the inevitable questions about his past life. His neighbours assumed he had taken his desk job for the benefits or the vacation time (some guessing at a sad past too, but such thoughts were unspoken) and these assumptions were fine with Polk. Micah was a happy distraction from the emptiness he felt in his chest, a child who went to school and played baseball. He was friends with the neighbourhood kids and so Polk knew their parents, but not intimately. He knew them enough to know Micah was safe, and the other parents knew the same about him. He could at least discuss the hobbies of their children amiably enough to pass the time while waiting for Micah to tie his shoes or find his baseball glove so they could go home and eat dinner together, a pleasure they shared every evening.

Micah was eleven on an afternoon he trailed his baseball bat along the hardwood floor and shouted upstairs to his father, *Pop, you got a letter,* and threw the pile of bills on the old table with the letter on top. It was from the government, and since Polk was a dedicated taxpayer he felt no fear or surprise until he read its curt message: *Your status has come to the attention of the government and you are to be deported. Please do not leave your place of residence and cooperate with all subsequent investigations. You will be notified of all procedures and the ongoing status of your application. Thank you for your cooperation in this matter.* There was a signature but it was illegible, and a legit-looking government insignia followed.

This was a joke: the letter was, Polk thought, poorly written. And of course Polk was Canadian. He was born in a small Catholic hospital in 1964, shortly after his parents immigrated to Canada. But he was orphaned young and lived in foster-care, never learning his heritage. He had a social insurance number; his birth certificate was lost but he had never left the country. It was also a dirty secret (it shamed Polk) that he had never married Micah's mother, although they were soul-mates. And while these were tolerable times in Canada, Polk certainly did not want Micah to know he was a bastard child. In fact, this is what Micah feared more than the ominous deportation itself (which now seemed less a joke), although Polk had not the slightest idea where he was being deported or why... *Illegitimacy,* he thought near tears, *as though that could have you banished.* It was no joke at all.

Micah, supper, come down, he said, and he carried on as before so Micah would not suspect anything. But of course nothing was the same. He watched Micah eat as the food on his own plate cooled. He thought about hiding, about where they would go, and he froze in disbelief: *I have failed my son.*

Two weeks later Polk received a second letter: his case was "under review." Polk began wearing sunglasses so the boy would not recognize his father's alarm. All around him, order remained—the placid veneer of the neighbourhood parents became impenetrable to Polk. He began to wonder about his desk job. At night he dreamed of voluptuous women who climbed out of his closet and into his bed. The sudden allure of orgasms pulled Polk away from the green neighbourhood and peaceful family life.

Polk's burden became too great. He needed to tell someone, and he decided on Mrs. Purse, a neighbourhood mother who was shaped like a curvy laundry-detergent bottle and who smelled twice as fragrant. Micah and her boy played baseball with one another, so Polk waited until they had picked up and gone off together to take the moment for confronting Mrs. Purse. He knocked.

Mrs. Purse, hello, he said. *Please, may I come in?*

Mrs. Purse stared at him as though he were the devil. Polk stared at Mrs. Polk, who had a dark chocolate smear across her upper lip and on her fingers. She had been caught indulging. She flushed.

Polk! Yes, of course. Yes, oh, but I'm a bit of a mess. I wasn't expecting—

Yes, yes, said Polk, who thought he knew too well what she was talking about. He did not take off his shoes in the hallway. In the kitchen, a half-tray of brownies sat on the island, where Mrs. Purse motioned for Polk to take a seat on a stool. In a smooth motion she slid the tray off the island, opened the fridge, and hid the chocolate.

I am going to lose my desk job, Polk sobbed.

Oh dear, said Mrs. Purse, who knew from her own husband that losing a desk job was serious, if not the worst thing that could happen. Polk's sorrow made her feel a little better about the chocolate, and she opened the fridge and pulled out the tray again, this time offering a piece to Polk, who accepted. She wiped the chocolate off her fingers with a napkin.

This is all I have, said Polk.

Mrs. Purse, who thought he was still talking about the desk job, sat beside him and patted his shoulder. *That is not true, Polk. There is always Micah. There is always the neighbourhood.*

The neighbourhood, Polk echoed. Then, embarrassed, he stifled his sobs and wheezed. He looked up into Mrs. Purse's face. She still wore her chocolate moustache. Polk tried not to stare. Mrs. Purse remembered the moustache, but she did not dare wipe it off now, in front of Polk. Her face glistened with sweat as Polk tried to turn away.

I'll have another chocolate, said Polk.

Yes, yes, said Mrs. Purse, red at the accusation.

TALMUD

Yes! She was not balding and she had excellent fashion sense. She had not lost her husband to poker, or her only daughter to a burlesque-revival show in Chicago. All truths, but not for Lilly, who could contort any fact into falsehood. It was delusion that inspired Lilly to sell her split-level Canadian home, pack two suitcases (crammed with bikinis and lacy bras) and move to Europe, where she had sensuous affairs with thirteen European men before birthing a child and returning to Canada, alone, to live in a small log cabin on the western shore of Lake Erie.

The European men refused to wear condoms because they were too thin for amorous European sex (of thirteen kinds, including Spanish, French, and Slovakian), and the pleasure too significantly reduced. She became pregnant. The boy was named Talmud and she left him with his father, Iran, a portly cigar-and-American pop-culture aficionado who was actually Russian-American and not foreign in the least. She wrote Iran a cheque for five thousand dollars and promised to send more. He

was happy to live his new American Dream of the dot-
ing single father, but in Amsterdam. He hugged Talmud
against his chest (the child crying at the force, but releas-
ing only a murmur against chiselled pectorals) as Lilly
boarded an airplane to New York and shouted a prom-
ise that Talmud should visit her when he turned twenty
and she had adjusted again to the notion of motherhood.

The trip left her breathless and yearning for genuine
peace. Although she was happier, the youthful vigor of
her European excursion depleted her energy and financial resources. Lilly did not know how to live a small-
town life. She bought a hatchback and drove it spar-
ingly. She lit her sparse lakeshore cabin with candles of
all manners, sizes, and scents. She bought a body pillow
to simulate the presence of another being beside her.
She applied for a job as a waitress of a faux-fifties diner
on the town's main drag and dressed every morning in
a checkered vinyl skirt. She eked out a living and grew
older.

After three years she felt cervical pain and sought
the town gynecologist, but he was stymied. The pain
increased and her hair thinned further; in the mirror she
saw patches of her scalp. She wore hats before realizing
it was a useless charade. She quit the diner and stayed

home whenever possible, read histories and biographies of famous and less-famous celebrities and politicians, and walked along the lake with her feet in wet sand, wishing she could bury herself in it.

During this period she received her first visitor who knew of both Iran and Talmud. He arrived suddenly, without luggage. He might have been sent, Lilly thought. His name was Pahl, he was from Norway, and he said Iran was a very good friend. Iran had indeed told him he would find Lilly here if he ever travelled in Canada. Talmud was beginning school and could write his and his mother's name very legibly. This made her happy. She slept with Pahl, *fucked him silly*, as she thought it, and it dulled her uterine pain. In the day, they stayed apart, each doing their own business. At such times Pahl was less a visitor than a guest in need of a room. That was fine with Lilly, who still did not desire permanent human kinship.

In the evenings they played Scrabble and then they fucked. And in the morning she went to the white beach. When the sheets were humid and tangled she sometimes asked him about Talmud. What else might he know? *Nothing,* he would say, *Iran has told me nothing else. Besides, what interest do I have in your child?* When Pahl left, citing a need *to see,* she felt lonely for Talmud.

In her seclusion she gained weight and lost more hair. She was nearly bald except for a ring of auburn hair that ran from ear-to-ear. Her water storage tanks were unreliable and she cut her bathing schedule to twice a week to conserve water. Her skin felt dirty and she neglected to shave her legs, her underarms, or the dark hair that began growing on her chin and above her upper lip. Her face, always large for her body but pretty, squared.

She received another visitor, Anders, who arrived in a pickup truck and was as burly and rank a man as she had known. She badly wanted to sleep with him. Her memory of Pahl faded, but Talmud still tumbled in pieces from her mouth.

Anders could not be forgotten. His odour was strong. When he came in her he squeezed so she felt her ribs crack, and he broke the couch he slept on with his girth. While Anders might have been large, he was so ubiquitously large in every aspect that he lacked any other quality of physical distinction or heritage. His eyebrows were neither thick nor thin, his hair neither dark nor light; if she pictured his face in a crowd along Times Square, or maybe a music festival, she would not recognize him at all were it not for his grandiosity, his burden. At the kitchen where she made him meals of ham and eggs, trays of toast, or basted turkeys and yams, she would prod him. *What are you*, she said, and clarified it quickly before he could be insulted: *I mean, where are you from, or your parents? Are you Hungarian? Yes*, he said. *I am Hungarian. Is that all you are?* Lilly asked. *No, I am also Swedish. I am American, and Icelandic, and Hungarian, and Swedish.* Lilly was afraid to ask him more because she was sure that he was more than she knew. Each new bit of information she received from him frightened her. *Swedish?* How so, she saw nothing of it in him. She could see nothing of anything in him other than his big pomposity. So he was not someone to ask anything of, not seeming to be anything himself. She never asked him about her son or told him what Pahl had known, that the boy could write his name. (Lilly desperately wanted Talmud to send a postcard with his name on it.)

Anders spent a time there, the particular length of which she could not remember, but when he prepared to return to Switzerland he mentioned that Iran was now living there with Talmud, who was beginning the third grade. He said it quickly, without so much as a head turn. Lilly was scarcely sure she heard him. He wrote her a cheque for the room. *No, no money required,* she said, *I'm not an inn. Don't be ridiculous.* But his truck and his largesse, so slowly importuned, were gone.

Lilly no longer had any use for dresses, for bras or stockings, and so discarded them. Her breasts adapted to their new freedom and shrunk against her chest. She rarely saw anyone and had no one to compare herself with, but she felt taller. Her shoulders were broader. She was comfortable urinating anywhere on the secluded beach or in the clumps of trees. In the absence of guests she was perfectly alone and *free*; and those words which had harmed her were now very different. Her voice was coarse. She put out the candles, tired of their scents. The uterine pain ceased.

Iran, the Russian-American in Switzerland, never wrote her with news of his own, of Talmud, but she still sent money for the child. But the cheques became smaller. She was out of work, and out of sorts with herself, as the saying went, in her physical body and soul. What was there to do? *Little, and littler still....* The travellers' cheques were reduced to two and three cents each, but she could ill-afford the international cheques and eventually mailed personal cheques. And when she felt she could order no more cheque books (and see the carbons of how little she was providing her abandoned son) she sent IOU's on sticky refrigerator notes. Freedom she had, and a body whose androgyny released her to feel whatever she wanted, to express it too: she could curl on a swinging chair in the deck and push the remnants of her breasts against her knees and rock herself like a child (or a mother rocking a child) or she could cut timber, pound her fists against the stumps, and walk through the forests bare-foot.

Win was very slender, effeminate, and of Thai descent. He did not announce himself until he closed the cabin door and said *My name is Win, and I was told I could board here.* He was short and fragile and moved with such grace that he mesmerized Lilly. He spoke softly and ate tofu. If he noticed her appearance it was unimportant or common. (Had he seen anyone else like her? This was a question she wanted to ask: could there be anyone *else*?) Win was, however, difficult to talk to. When he touched her it was a faint tickle, and when he left the house the doors never slammed. When he cooked meals, the silverware did not clank, the blender did not whirr, and knives never clunked against the cutting board. Win said little too, but Lilly suspected he, like the others, had news of Talmud. Win said he was on a tour of North America and that he was enamoured with the Great Lakes. But he would not tell her anything else, not easily. *Seduce me,* he said, *and I will tell you.*

For the first time in her life Lilly seduced a man. There was no trick to it, none that she remembered reading about in the magazines or had seen in television movies. Win drifted in and out of the cabin, and she would wait for him to come back, yet whenever he entered a room she was caught off-guard by his silence. Then she would grab him and motion toward the bed, but he said *That is not right, that is not how you do it.* She tried, but Win continually said that it was wrong. She grew tired of his rejections and one morning threw Win on the bed. He moaned. She bit his wrists and pushed his body into a prone position. She could not remember who entered who but the sensation was fiery and as deep-nerved a pain as she had known, not unlike child-birth. When it was over Win became withdrawn and contemplative. *Where the fuck's my son?* Lilly demanded. *I do not know*, protested Win, *I have not heard.* Lilly picked him up and threw him on the porch. *Get the fuck off my property.*

She spent entire days walking along the beaches past other cottages on the white sand of the beach. The fat which had made her so much larger tightened into mus-cle. Her hands grew rough with the work of keeping the cabin. She admitted she knew little of fatherhood, but her attitudes toward motherhood were reconciled.

She went to the department store and bought several large flannel shirts, jeans, and a pair of boots, sold the car and the cabin, bought a plane ticket for Switzerland, and followed the trail suggested by her European visitors. She found Iran, who was much smaller and more beautiful than she remembered, at a spa in Tribschen. He wore a long, flowing muumuu, the fabric trailing past the drainpipes by the sauna. They fucked in the dense steam (where they could not see each other) before Iran offered to take Lilly home. Talmud could at long last meet the father they had abandoned when they fled North America, which he did with two small eyes peeking out from the bottom of Iran's dress, the hem held above his head.

JURISPRUDENCE

Liza Baptist's husband John, a teacher, was released from the hospital because it was his wish to die at home. Liza wanted to repaint their bedroom a tranquil blue to calm him, and put on the table fresh flowers and greeting cards friends and students sent for comfort. She was unemployed and had little else to do but dwell. He refused, wanting instead to die in the room he had slept in for twenty years, as familiar and comforting as the smell of his wife's moisturizers. He needn't have left the hospital if he wanted a change and where he was going would be change enough. Liza left the room dull as her husband asked, but stayed constantly by his side and radiated pleasantness by fluffing his pillows or changing his sheets. The doctors said he could go at any time and as horrible as it was, this was not like a dental appointment or some other inconvenience to be accidentally missed or avoided.

On the white pillow his bald head resembled an egg on a piece of china. He lay on his back and sang bits of songs he knew to keep himself thinking and acting alive. In a lucid moment he said: *You never hear of nuns going senile,* which was sensible, figuring they spent their days reciting prayers. *Too, you never hear of them losing their cool on their deathbed, saying things they wish not to say.*

But when the pain was too great he half-closed his eyes and his speech trailed into strings of deluded chatter. Liza didn't mind; the babbles were more pleasing than the laboured breathing of his sleep. Because they had no children of their own Liza bought a baby monitor and kept it about her while she did the laundry or the cooking. Her husband's chatter was random but articulate and kept her company when she felt most alone.

After one week Liza felt her impatience as keenly as her sadness. Death had anchored in their house and refused to unshore. She was no longer radiant at his side. Wiping sweat off her husband's forehead was a chore and so too were the tedious acts of feeding and bathing. In the kitchen or laundry his murmuring was comforting, reminding her he was alive. When she heard him gurgle his songs it almost made her think that he relied on her by choice and not necessity. But in the flesh he was unbearable. She was expectantly sad, but also repulsed by his condition and her reactions to its malevolence. She adopted a strict schedule of feeding, bathing, idle conversation (in which she discussed the news of her day while he wet himself or groaned or slept) and patient sitting. She kept her schedule to the minute and when it was over she ran down the stairs, even if she was mid-sentence or if a rare kiss was interrupted. But more often she finished what she had to say a minute or two before and waited out the clock before leaving the room, never searching her husband's face for any kind of permission or understanding.

Thus she relied on her baby monitor and always kept it about her, the volume as loud as it would go so she could understand him. And although she imagined he was hurt, he also must have understood, for they began to have all their moments of conversation over the intercom, and, after that, even their moments of waiting together; she would say, *It's okay, John, I'm here, in the living room,* and he would stop murmuring as they shared a moment together but apart. *It is,* she broke the crackling silence once, *a trial separation.* Then: *baby steps.* They saw each other only at the designated bathing, feeding, and sheet-changing times.

On the ninth day the monitor batteries died and Liza broke the strict schedule to tell him she was going to leave the house to buy another set. *Get some groceries, too,* he said. She went as fast as she could, and she fit the batteries in their socket of the monitor as she drove back home. With the monitor off he might as well already be dead. Down the street or across dimensions, it made no difference. (Awful thinking.) The crackling static whirred loudly as she pulled into the driveway. She heard a croak muttering a name, which she thought was *Edward Talli-burton, a barrister,* and then a very horrible silence. She turned the radio as loud as it would go in hopes of pick-ing up his shallow breaths. But either the monitor had fallen off the bed and was on the floor, or her husband was dead.

She thought it was very bad for her to break the schedule for the second time in the same day, and it was not even ten o'clock. Maybe that was why he was dead, or perhaps his attachment to life was never more power-ful than the thin current coursing through the monitor. Liza knelt by him and, stricken with grief, put her head on the bed sheet although he had soiled himself some-time before dying. *John,* she said, *I said don't die before I come home. That was the least you could do.*

In stories of death this is an unmentioned part. After she grieved inconsolably for nearly twenty minutes, Liza had no idea what to do next. Who to call, who to notify —even if she should pull the sheets over his head like they did on medical dramas, or put her husband on the floor so she could change him and leave his body in a state of decency before a higher authority arrived. But decency, she figured, was only mortal. She remembered Edward Talliburton, Barrister, and looking at her watch saw the allotted time for sitting or waiting was over.

She found the barrister's business address unremarkably enough. It was on a major thoroughfare in the city's north end, an old row of bungalows converted into dentists' and pediatricians' offices, internet service providers, and massage therapy clinics. She asked the burly secretary to see Edward Talliburton, Barrister, and after giving her name she was shown into a tiny waiting area that must have once been a laundry room or a room of some another utilitarian function. The barrister's office was undecorated save for the requisite degrees and file cabinet. On his desk were two pencils, a pad of legal paper and an old computer. On the large uncovered space lay his two hands, immense, thick and spread-fingered. He stood to greet her and was very tall. Liza was self-conscious that he might see down her blouse or notice a red scar on the top of her head. But he seemed benevolent and smiled broadly, revealing very large teeth.

I am Edward Talliburton, Barrister, he said. Liza reached out and shook his hand. It enveloped hers completely and warmed it. His flesh was red and oily. She introduced herself.

Your husband, yes, he said. *It is very sad, he was an old friend.*

She asked him how he knew her husband, and the answer provided was long and vague and miffed her. It involved friends of friends, and roommates, a college dorm, a party, and some volunteer function. It was a long list of name-dropping, some of whom she knew, many she did not. And yet he seemed to know that her husband was dead although Liza had not told him.

He has, said Edward Talliburton, Barrister, *completed a will and testament and asked me to discuss the details with you.* He rose and moved toward the filing cabinet. Seeing a constipated look on her face he stopped, saying, *If it is not prudent to do so now, we may wait, of course.* He sat back down. *Why are you here?*

Her voice rising in pitch she told him of her husband's illness and his last days at home, which she had hoped to make comfortable for him but had instead made comfortable for herself. And how, in her selfishness, she had instructed him not to die until she could be with him as he left, and how his dying without her was also selfish and unforgivable. Throughout, the barrister was attentive and silent. When she finished and brushed her short hair behind her ears with a mournful gesture indicating she had said her piece, the large Edward Talliburton, Barrister, unfurled his crossed arms and said:

What would you say if I told you something… that I can bring your husband, briefly, back?

She asked how and he sighed loudly.

It is a possibility.

Then, she said, *my husband won't die alone.*

No, said the barrister, *that will not happen.*

He won't, however, amended the barrister, *be coherent. He has already seen the light beyond. God wouldn't find it prudent to enable the reborn to discuss what they had seen in the afterlife.* Liza agreed; it had been a long time since John was significantly coherent. Edward Talliburton, Barrister, said the secretary would handle the paperwork. She could go home.

We must, he said, *discuss the will when you return.*

The dark thought did little to sully Liza's jubilance, and she nodded.

Tell your husband, said the barrister, *I say hello.*

As she neared the house the baby monitor whistled and whined. Pulling into the driveway, she heard a muffled cough and a gasp for *water.* She filled a small sipping cup with ice and water and bounded up the stairs. Her husband was breathing, but the room stank of his filth. *Here,* she said, tenderly raising his chin and pouring a sip into his mouth. She continued for several sips until John closed his mouth when she pressed the spout to his lips. The magic of his return abated, she placed the cup on the nightstand then punched him rather heavily in the stomach. *I told you not to leave me!* she screamed, and she cried, *You have no idea what it is like to be left alone!*

Yelling at him made both of them, she thought, feel normal again, like their relationship was not one based on dependency. He was stoic and unanswering as he had always been, but her haranguing was the closest thing to an argument they had in the year since John's diagnosis. John did not speak at all, and thus without delusion; he must have been incoherent, like the barrister had said he would, but his eyes were clear and white, and the sun through the blind barred his face with bands of light and dark. He looked at her, not the ceiling, captivated by the magnanimity of her assaulting emotions. And, she saw, he looked more than a little sad.

Edward Talliburton, Barrister, says hello, she said as if to explain why he was back from the dead and in their old plain room. *He told me a lot of things I don't know about*

*you, John. While I know you can't answer you have no idea
how terrible it feels to think that the husband I love so dearly
has secrets to keep!*

She stayed with him much longer than any allotted
schedule. What other secrets were there? Had he been
with other women? Why did he not tell her about the
will? He had said he wanted no children. Was that a lie?
John offered no head shrugs or shakes to suggest he
understood. He was ashen and his skin was hardening
by the moment. He lay frozen against the sheets. The
sun had settled and the venetian bands of lights covered
the lumps of his belly and thighs. Liza wanted simply to
be happy her husband was here with her again, betray-
ing the rules of physics if only for a while. But the
gnawing distrust and anger filled her with questions
asking further questions. She shouted at him, then
talked to him calmly, and then sat in the chair beside the
bed and counted how many laboured breaths he took
each moment.

You're going to leave me again, she said. But he was
asleep. Edward Talliburton's fantastic abilities had caused
her to suspect everyone's motives and abilities. One of
the suspicions which repeated itself was that she had
done something to deserve this: it was all a trick com-
mitted out of bad taste. John had been, at times, that

kind of man. Then she thought that was a horrible thing to think of a dying husband, who deserved a proper eulogy. And although she knew time was growing thin she went to the kitchen to boil water for tea and think about what she wanted to say. The water boiled and the whistling blotted the monitor as a last sound croaked. She had, like many other wives, missed her husband's passing, but she was certain she was the only wife to miss it twice. How he likely hated her, and she had no idea! His passing into death might have made his hate for her permanent and irrevocable; if there was an afterlife (Liza was not entirely sure she believed, but even so) she would be denied a potential reunion with her husband. She had loved him, and he her, she knew, once, perhaps if only in the earliest years, when they lived in a row of townhouses on a pullout bed, her husband's face as babyish as his students. He was so beautiful! And what did she know?

She went back to Edward Talliburton, Barrister. *Tell me,* she said, *about my husband.*

There is the matter of the will, he said, *which we did not discuss in our first meeting, giving the prudence of making quick amends.* His large face, oblique and squared as a cinder block, moved very little as he spoke. He studied her quivering face. She looked as she might fall if he talked loud enough. *I suspect*, he said, *your efforts at a rec-onciliatory peace were not successful?*

No, she had failed, she told him. And she told him about everything she had done and said to him, and how he had again died without her. *And you want to bring him back, again?* he asked. She had not thought of that. *Yes,* she said, without surety. He asked *Why*, and the interrogation pierced her resolve and she collapsed into the chair. *Let's look at the will,* said Edward Talliburton, Barrister.

This was the big secret she had dreaded. John had not told her about any will but one had been drafted, it was true—it was in front of her in a large brown file. It was typed in long incomprehensible clauses, and as Edward Talliburton, Barrister, explained it to her, he pointed at specific lines with fingers that might have popped Liza's head like a pimple. The revelation of this secret was magical, but it was, she thought, not all in the impenetrable secret of the will. It was in Edward Talli-burton, who Liza could not pummel on the stomach while breaking into grievous tears. No matter how real he was, how malodourous his breath (and it steamed out of him in great gasps as he illumined the dark brush of text), the rules of their conduct and civility were more tightly wound than any legal contract or even Liza and

John's own marriage vows. How powerful! And yet silly, that the social civility of polite conversation and service between two people could be so ironclad, and a marriage so porous. His voice consoled and croaked in froggy tones. He shifted in his chair and it creaked.

My goodness, was all she could think to say.

Edward Talliburton, Barrister, continued: John had come into a large sum of money some time shortly after he and Liza first met, a gift from a wild and terminally ill aunt who had bequeathed him a tidy twenty thousand. He then contacted the barrister, who had wrapped the secret in a pile of pages. So John had known the barrister nearly as long as he had known her. How terrible! Liza asked why she had not heard of this and Edward Talliburton, Barrister, said: *Wait a moment, Mrs. Baptist. The inheritance is conditional,* and the condition was the money was to go to a child. If there was no child, it was to go to a reputable charity for terminally ill children.

A child, she said, and she was confused. They had no children but John had never particularly expressed such a desire—in their early years he loved a good fuck, of course, like men in general, which Liza knew too. But the children of his classes brought enough joy into his life, and no man, he said, wants to take his work home with him, if he can help it. That was not how he said it, but it was the intention. She had not wanted children at all, and she had ignored the light in his eyes when they spoke of the children. And so he said he did not want his own although he had given the students his love, and theirs to him. As the disease paled him and put rings under his eyes, as it ate his once fleshy thighs and soured his appetites and lusts, he changed into a new, unknowable person, impenetrable as the will however politely and regrettably, as in his verbal delusions. So he had wanted children perhaps, at least after the onset, and she recalled one night, after John was first diagnosed, that they *had* had a good fuck, or at least what passed for one then. She had dropped the birth control, so she unwrapped a condom to pull down on his cock (perhaps, she thought, like one of his students might tug on his or her boot to walk to school), and he had murmured, *No, it's okay, Liza, leave it off.* He came so softly she hardly felt it.

If I have a child, she said, *he will have the money.*

If you had, said the barrister, trailing off.

But you can bring him back, she said.

For you, he replied, *I will once more. After that, I fear the paperwork will become complicated.*

She left the radio off as she drove home because she trusted that Edward Talliburton, Barrister, would be good to his word. He had known John as long as she had, and between them that was a good number of years to make Edward Talliburton trustworthy, perhaps a great deal more than her husband. She didn't know what she thought of John anymore, but she didn't worry much about it. He had ceased being John since he had lived and died more than once.

John was awake and shaking in his bed. She flung off the sheets. Sweat pooled behind his head, back and rear; it was a great lake of odourless perspiration (how long had it been since he had made a motion worthy of an earthy sweat?). He was muttering: he spouted lines from movies he had seen, and a line from the Lord's Prayer. For a long moment she stood by him holding his hand. She understood now that it was useless to talk to him. She looked into his eyes and waited for a response that might have said *go ahead*; when she received a head loll that suggested what she wanted to see, she reached under the sheet and began to work over her husband. How warm he felt between her hands! How good that was, alive, ruddy, and complexioned so unlike the rest of his body; indeed it must never have died. How she missed and loved him! She continued her work and climbed on top of the bed and rode him as gently as she could, though each sound of the springs told her she was overworking him. One last good fuck before his third death would do him good. Did Edward Talliburton agree? But she tried to stop that thought.

To her surprise he did finish, and without the latex she felt the nearly imperceptible lunge. She climbed off as slow as she could to not disturb him, kissed him on the cheek, and ran downstairs for water. She ran back upstairs and put her head on her husband's breast and counted the minutes until he died. He died within the half-hour.

He was gone at last but she felt somewhat reconciled. She had the body picked up and arranged the funeral services, which went off as well as could be hoped. She studied the many faces of sad children who held their parents' hands at the receptions. How morbid, she thought, that their parents let them come. She waited to empty the house of his things partly out of the knowledge that she should be grieving him (although the urge had been exhumed) and partly because she wanted some sense of him here if she was pregnant. Two weeks later she took the test: she was. She was elated: in nine months a tiny part of her husband would be back! And she would have the money.

She went to the barrister. It was warm and she felt very good about everything: the composure with which she had buried him, and the calm thought which had given her the supreme idea of sleeping with him one last time. It was the best for both of them and now there would be a child and a resurrection, the child she had never known she had wanted. That was a deep kind of love, that desire to love and not know it.

She told the barrister the good news, but for the first time in their two encounters (it was odd how, in her mind, it seemed as they had known each other for twenty years) he was agitated and not present, not in control. *What is wrong?* she asked. He shook his head and said:

This is all very new, Liza, it is only recently passed.

Liza did not understand.

The law has never heard of a man dying three times before. I tried to stop you, to slow you down, to wait. Wait out death? Her husband had been dying, there was no time to wait, she was getting old, her death was likely not far off and loneliness was crawling like a worm into her soul. And she had been ostracized by her husband's secrecy of the will and money. What time? And then there never could have been a child, John could not be revived. She did not know, she knew nothing about the legislation. It was all hocus-pocus by the magical Edward Talliburton, Barrister, who was more conjurer than barrister. How eager she had been to believe everything he had told her. The barrister had resumed talking but stopped short and, in an unbarrister-like gesture, rose from behind his desk to hug her. *Marriage,* she murmured to the barrister, *is a terrible thing for lonely people.* But the only sound was a squeezed sigh, soft enough to be lost in the ventilation, her body a dead weight.

ACKNOWLEDGEMENTS

With warmest affection I thank Priscila Uppal, Christopher Doda, and Richard Teleky for their large hearts and literary sensibilities. Without Meaghan Strimas, her unflinching eye, and editorial flair, this work would be half as good and twice as long.

Thanks also to Michael and Barry Callaghan, who ignored my arrears. Christian Bok and Susan Swan taught me a thing or two hundred about writing. Tanya MacIntosh and Emrys Davis offered early advice on these stories. Shannon MacNeill and Brendan Narancsik didn't mind sharing a house with a moody writer. Two dozen colleagues took friendly hacks at "Matchbook for a Mother's Hair," and I'm a better writer for their efforts.

Collie Pamplona, I have not forgotten you.

I apologize to anyone if I glazed over mid-conversation in the past three years. I assure you I was only writing this book.

I am indebted to the Ontario Arts Council and the Writer's Trust / McClelland & Stewart "Journey Prize" for their financial support.

Warm thanks also to the family of Mike and Joanne Pautler, for their acceptance and good humour.

Not least, I thank my family, Ernie, Lise, and Michael.

And Cat, who has always let the horse eat the violin.

The epigraph was culled from Bertrand Russell's *A History of Western Philosophy*.

"Anecdote of the Jar" is for Wallace Stevens and his poem of the same title.

"Dreschl & The Obvious Child" is for Georges Perec. The character of Alphonse Andolph is dedicated to Bernard Malamud.

"Matchbook for a Mother's Hair," "Anecdote of the Jar," and "Dreschl & the Obvious Child" previously appeared in *Exile: The Literary Quarterly.*

"Matchbook for a Mother's Hair" also appeared in *The Journey Prize Stories: 17,* and went on to be selected as the winner of the *$10,000 Journey Prize* in 2006.